BENEATH THE
SWIRLING SKY

THE RESTORATIONISTS

BENEATH THE SWIRLING SKY

by

CAROLYN LEILOGLOU

ILLUSTRATIONS BY VIVIENNE TO

WATERBROOK

BENEATH THE SWIRLING SKY

Text copyright © 2023 by Carolyn Leiloglou

Cover art and interior illustrations copyright © 2023 by Vivienne To

Excerpt from *Between Flowers and Bones* by Carolyn Leiloglou
© 2024 by Carolyn Leiloglou.

Published in the United States by WaterBrook, an imprint of Random House,
a division of Penguin Random House LLC.

WATERBROOK and colophon are registered trademarks
of Penguin Random House LLC.

Hardback ISBN 978-0-593-57952-7
Trade Paperback ISBN 978-0-593-57954-1
Ebook ISBN 978-0-593-57953-4

Library of Congress Cataloging-in-Publication Data
Names: Leiloglou, Carolyn, author.
Title: Beneath the swirling sky / by Carolyn Leiloglou.
Description: First edition. | Colorado Springs : WaterBrook, [2023]
Identifiers: LCCN 2022033518 |
ISBN 9780593579527 (hardcover) | ISBN 9780593579534 (ebook)
Subjects: CYAC: Secret societies—Fiction. | Magic—Fiction. | Painting—Fiction. |
Brothers and sisters—Fiction. | Fantasy. | LCGFT: Fantasy fiction. | Novels.
Classification: LCC PZ7.1.L4558 Be 2023 | DDC [Fic]—dc23
LC record available at https://lccn.loc.gov/2022033518

Printed in the United States of America

waterbrookmultnomah.com

10 9 8 7 6 5 4

First Edition

Cover design by Ashley Tucker

Book design by Jen Valero

SPECIAL SALES Most WaterBrook books are available at special quantity discounts
when purchased in bulk by corporations, organizations, and special-interest
groups. Custom imprinting or excerpting can also be done to fit special needs.
For information, please email specialmarketscms@penguinrandomhouse.com.

TO CAMPBELL,
YOU WERE CALLED TO CREATE—
NEVER STOP MAKING ART!

Every child is an artist.
The problem is how to remain an artist
once he grows up.

—PABLO PICASSO

There's something of Rembrandt in the Gospels
or of the Gospels in Rembrandt, as you wish,
it comes to more or less the same.

—VINCENT VAN GOGH

1

Vincent should have been spending spring break at the beach or Knott's Berry Farm or at least having a video-game marathon with his friends. Instead, he was staring out the backseat window at the endless Texas countryside rolling by. He let his eyes unfocus, and the field, cows, and clumps of short trees blurred like an impressionist painting. But painting—or rather, not painting—was what had gotten him into this mess. Mom thought she was being subtle about it, but Vincent knew the only reason she and Dad had booked a cruise out of Galveston instead of Los Angeles, where they lived, was her "secret" plan to reconnect him with art. Mom wanted Vincent and his sister, Lili, to meet her uncle Leo, who was some kind of art restorer.

Not just meet but stay with him for the whole week of spring break.

In the middle-of-nowhere Texas with no cell service.

At least when her plan failed, Mom might finally quit bugging him to paint again.

When Mom and Dad had sprung this plan on them, Vincent had tried to talk his way out of it. They'd never even met Mom's extended family. Mom had just sighed and responded that sometimes family is complicated. Lili, of course, had instantly added Uncle Leo to the family tree she was making for school, right alongside Vincent, Mom, Dad, and the birth parents she had never met.

Vincent smiled at the memory. Lili was always ready to welcome someone new, though she hadn't always been that way. Three years ago, when Vincent was nine, his parents had adopted three-year-old Lili from China. They'd spent almost two weeks with her in China, and then finally, on the day before they needed to fly home, Lili had clutched Vincent's hand, refusing to let go. Some siblings didn't get along, but Vincent and Lili had been close ever since that moment, even though it had taken a while before they spoke the same language.

"I'm amazed you can still find this place without GPS," Dad said as Mom pulled off the two-lane road onto a gravel drive.

Vincent got his first glimpse of his great-uncle Leo's two-story white ranch house. It stood alone in a field dotted with red and blue wildflowers. Vincent felt like he'd been dropped in an endless world on *Minecraft*, minus the ability to build.

"Remember," Mom said as they got out of the car, "your great-uncle does some very important art conservation he can tell you about, and he's got lots of beautiful paintings you can look at. But no touching the art." She gave Vincent a very serious look as if this were something he might actually be tempted to do. "Understand?"

"No problem." He wasn't planning on touching the art or doing anything else with it.

"I want to see all the pretty pictures," Lili said. She hopped up and down, her ever-present toy bunny, Mr. Rumples, tucked snugly under her arm.

"You can look at all the pictures that aren't in Uncle Leo's work studio. And there's lots to do outside. You can pick wildflowers, catch grasshoppers. There's even a river, but you should not go there without your brother. Vincent, please make sure to watch your sister." Mom sighed as she looked out across the field with the hint of a smile. "I used to love it here."

The front door burst open, and a thin man with wiry gray hair and a bushy white mustache strode toward them with arms stretched wide.

"Artemisia! Jeffery! How the heck are y'all?" His deep Texas drawl surprised Vincent. Mom had grown up nearby and didn't really have an accent. Did she use to talk like that?

Uncle Leo hugged Mom and shook Dad's hand before turning to Vincent and Lili. "Vincent! You remind me so much of your grandfather with those brown eyes." He clapped him on the shoulder, then squatted. "And you must be Lilias." He stuck out his hand for her to shake, and she gave him a high five. Vincent smiled while his parents tried to show Lili how to shake hands.

A laugh from the porch drew Vincent's attention. A tall girl in short overalls stood in the doorway. She looked about Vincent's age, with olive skin and short copper-red hair sticking up all over her head like she'd cut it herself. His own curly brown hair might be untamable, but at least he tried. She had a gray smear of *something* across her cheek, and more spots covered her arms and clothes like she'd just lost a mud fight to a pig. He wouldn't be caught dead in public looking like that. Even if there was barely anyone here to see him.

"Georgia," Uncle Leo called, waving her down to join them, "come meet your second cousins."

Vincent hadn't realized he had a second cousin, much less that he'd apparently be spending a week with her. Hopefully she wouldn't be as weird as she looked.

"Georgia! It's nice to finally meet you." Mom's fake-happy voice set Vincent on edge. She talked like that only when things weren't going the way she had planned but she didn't want anyone to know. She gathered Georgia into an awkward hug, but Vincent didn't miss the worried glance she shared with Dad over Georgia's shoulder. Yup, something was off here. "Uncle Leo didn't tell me you'd be here! Are your parents visiting as well?"

"No, ma'am, it's just me," Georgia responded. Now that she was closer, the spots on her face and arms definitely looked like mud.

"I see." Mom looked significantly at Uncle Leo. "Vincent, why don't you grab the bags? And, Georgia, do you mind helping them get settled while we have a little chat with your grandfather?"

Georgia nodded and jogged down to the car. "I can carry Lili's bag upstairs." She lifted Lili's flower-covered suitcase from the trunk.

She seemed nice enough, even if she looked like a homeless person. So why was Mom acting so jumpy? Something strange was going on.

Lili was talking nonstop as Georgia lugged her suitcase up the steps.

Vincent pulled his own bag slowly from the trunk, trying to eavesdrop as his mom spoke in an urgent whisper. He caught only two words—*traveling* and *involved*—but she sounded concerned.

"Wouldn't dream of getting him mixed up in it!" Uncle

Leo's booming voice didn't seem capable of whispering. "I already spoke to Georgia. She's not here to travel anyhow."

Travel? What was that supposed to mean? Mom seemed upset about Georgia *being* here, not that she would go somewhere else. Vincent rolled his suitcase toward the door as slowly as possible, trying to act oblivious to the conversation. Dad placed his arm around Mom's shoulder as if trying to comfort her, but Vincent couldn't make out her reply.

"Maybe she'll be a good influence on Vincent," Uncle Leo continued. "You wanted him to reconnect with art, right?"

Vincent rolled his eyes as he dragged his bag up the steps to the house. Mom's plan wasn't going to work. He was done with art for good, and sticking him on this ranch with perfect strangers wasn't going to help anything.

He paused at the top step, straining to hear just a little bit more.

"Do you want to cancel the cruise?" Dad asked. "I don't think we can get our deposit back, but—"

"No," Mom cut in. "As long as—"

"Vincent, come see the house!" Lili called, her voice drowning out the rest of Mom's reply.

Dad caught his eye, and Vincent knew he couldn't linger any longer without getting in trouble. But their conversation had left him with a nagging question: If his mom wanted him here to reconnect with art, what was it that she *didn't* want him involved in?

That question dropped from his mind the moment he stepped into Uncle Leo's house. Mom had said there'd be a lot of art, but this was ridiculous. Paintings were jigsawed together like a real-world *Tetris* game covering every inch of wall space in the entryway, into the next room, and even up the stairway. Some canvases were taller than him, and others were smaller than his phone. There were splotchy modern-art pieces, hazy impression-istic landscapes, hyper-realistic portraits, and every style in between. This was more art than he'd expect in a mu-seum, much less someone's home. And even weirder— not a single painting was framed. He shook his head. Art was the last thing he wanted to think about, but if every room was like this, there'd be nowhere to escape. This was going to be a long week.

"Never seen a painting before?" Georgia asked. A smirk played on her face as she stared down at him from the narrow staircase to his left. Lili stood next to her, lost in a painting.

Great. He'd already been caught looking at the art. Point one to Mom. "Not all crammed together like this." He tried to sound as uninterested as possible, but he couldn't help but ask, "Why aren't any of them framed?"

Georgia shrugged. "Reasons." He waited for her to add more, but she continued to stand at the top of the stairs, staring at him. She was so weird.

Lili, finally seeming to notice he was here, ran back down the stairs, grabbed Vincent's hand, and pulled him after her. "Come on! I want to see everything." She had Mr. Rumples clutched in her other hand, and to avoid looking at any more art, Vincent focused on the way the rabbit bounced against Lili's leg with each step.

The stairs led to a dim, narrow hallway that smelled old and stuffy. Three doors lined the left side, though only the first two were open. On the right was a row of sliding doors that Vincent assumed was storage space. Through the open door at the hall's end, he could make out a bathroom. The hallway was lit only by the dim evening light filtering in from the open doors, casting shadows on the walls.

"It's spooky up here." Lili stepped closer to Vincent and glued herself against his leg.

"That's because this is where the boogeyman lives!" Georgia made her eyes big and held up her hands like claws. "If you don't do as you're told, you'll vanish!"

"Really?" Lili tensed against Vincent's leg, fingers digging into his side. Vincent squeezed her shoulders.

"No, not really." Georgia dropped her hands and laughed. "Everything's just really old."

What was wrong with this girl? She might be weirder than this house. "It's not nice to scare little kids."

"I'm not little! I'm six!" Lili crossed her arms. Mr. Rumples dangled from one hand, as if challenging anyone to disagree.

"Sorry." Georgia gave a somewhat-apologetic shrug. "I'm not around other kids much. Not in person."

"What does that mean?" Vincent asked as Georgia rolled Lili's bag into the first room. "Don't you go to school?"

"I'm homeschooled." Georgia scooped a mound of clothes from one of the two single beds and tossed it into a corner. "But I travel with my parents so much that *road-schooled* is a better word. I've got some friends from a couple online classes, but we aren't ever in one place long enough to make many in-real-life friends. Plus, I'm an only child, so . . ." She shrugged again, like it was no big deal, but it sounded like a lonely way to live. Sure, school sometimes stunk, especially math, and Vincent didn't always enjoy Lili tagging along, but not having friends you could see most days sounded miserable.

Vincent glanced around the room as Lili, with Mr. Rumples, bounced onto the now-clear bed. The room looked very lived in, but at least there were no paintings. "How often do you stay here?"

"Pretty much any time I'm not traveling with my parents, so a lot. Come on, and I'll show you your room."

Lili continued to play with Mr. Rumples while Georgia walked back into the narrow hallway and gestured toward the room next door. Vincent stepped inside and took in the space. It was smaller, with a double bed against one wall and a desk and dresser against the other. Thankfully, this room was also painting-free.

"We'll have to share the bathroom. And if you get bored, the closets are always interesting." She slid open the door to one of the hall closets, revealing piles of junk: out-of-date clothes, lamps, broken chairs, old toys, and even a beat-up canoe.

Vincent stepped back into the hallway and glanced toward the one thing Georgia had failed to mention. "What's in there?" He pointed at the closed door.

"It's just . . ." Georgia glanced uncomfortably at the ceiling. "It's just locked. We're not supposed to go in there." Before Vincent could reply, she turned back to the room she was sharing with his sister. "Lili, do you want to see my wheel or look at art?"

"I want to see everything!" Lili said.

Wheel? Vincent pictured Georgia guiding his sister to a sinister spinning wheel like in a fairy tale. He was tempted to tell Lili not to touch the spindle, but that would be super weird.

Instead, he leaned in and whispered to Georgia, "No more scary stories, okay? Lili gets bad dreams."

"Got it." Georgia saluted him on her way down the stairs.

He couldn't figure her out. She acted odd, then nice, then clueless, then evasive. At least Lili seemed to like her, despite the boogeyman joke. But he wanted to find out why she made Mom uncomfortable.

He walked up to the closed room and jiggled the knob. Well, she wasn't lying about it being locked.

Vincent hugged his parents while Lili clung to Dad's leg like she wasn't going to let him go ever, until she got distracted by a yellow butterfly.

Vincent pulled out his phone. No bars, of course. He hadn't had reception for the last hour of their drive, so he'd need internet if he wanted to text or game with friends or anything. "What's the Wi-Fi, Uncle Leo?"

"The what now?" Uncle Leo's bushy eyebrows drew down, casting a shadow over his eyes.

"You know, Leo," Dad said. "For the internet. The password and all."

"Ahh, I have the World Wide Web on my PC in the

studio," Uncle Leo said, "but I can't have these kids running in and out of there. It's best to just use the telephone."

Georgia rolled her eyes. "Gramps only has dial-up."

Dad stifled a laugh.

"Oh no!" Mom said. "Then we won't be able to video chat with the kids while we're on the cruise!"

"What's dial-up?" Lili asked.

"It's like Stone Age internet," Georgia said.

Uncle Leo crossed his arms. "It's a waste of money when I already pay the phone bill. Anyone who wants to get ahold of me knows how."

Great. A week in middle-of-nowhere Texas surrounded by the very thing he didn't want to think about and no internet. At least he'd downloaded a couple of games onto his console before their trip.

"It's less than a week," Dad said. "It'll be good for you. Fresh air and all that."

"You'll find things to do. There's so much art to look at, and Uncle Leo can show you how he restores paintings," Mom said. "Boredom breeds creativity, right?"

By which she obviously meant "Start painting again." Not likely. And if there was anything else to do in an old house in the middle of nowhere with no internet, Vincent couldn't imagine what.

2

As his parents drove away, the girls ran off to pick wildflowers before the sun set. Vincent decided to see if he could get more info about Georgia from Uncle Leo. He didn't really want to look at the art as he stepped back into the house, but it was hard not to. He was surrounded! He slowed his steps, noticing for the first time that each painting had an index card thumbtacked underneath it. Each had the artist's name and painting title written in permanent marker, as if this were some kind of hick museum.

He froze when he read the name Henri Matisse under a painting of a woman in a chair who was shading herself with a red umbrella. Matisse was famous. Like, museum famous. Regular people didn't own paintings by Matisse. He glanced at the next painting, a self-portrait by Frida Kahlo, another super-famous artist. He read a few more index cards, recognizing many of the artists' names. With an art teacher for a mom, it was hard not to know who these people were. But how did Uncle Leo come to have all these famous artists crowded along the walls of his home? Vincent paused, mesmerized, in front of a forested landscape by Paul Cézanne. The colors . . . the way the brushstrokes blended together . . . He'd never been so close to a *real* painting before—well, other than his own, back when he used to paint—and he never could have been this good, even if he'd practiced a hundred years.

Vincent felt a deep tug inside his gut. If only things could have been different. If he'd been able to . . . But no. That part of him was over now.

His eyes wandered to a surreal landscape by Georgia O'Keeffe. That must be the artist his second cousin was named after. It was pretty weird, like his cousin, so the name kind of fit her. He hadn't thought about their family naming tradition in a long time, but Mom had told him that each child in their family was named after a great artist. He was named after Vincent van Gogh, and his sister after little-known artist Lilias Trotter. Uncle Leo must be named after Leonardo da Vinci. His mom's name was Artemisia, after an Italian painter. She had a sister whose name also started with an *A*, but Vincent couldn't remember it or her, since she died when

Vincent was a baby. As he took in the art around him, he wondered how that tradition started.

A flash of movement caught his eye, drawing his attention back to the forest painting. He took a step closer. It looked so lifelike. He could almost see the wind blowing the trees, feel it brushing his face.

"Keep your paws off the art!"

Vincent blinked as if coming out of a trance. He glanced in horror at his right hand, which hovered in front of the painting, inches away from grazing its surface. Vincent dropped his arm and swung to face Uncle Leo, whose bushy eyebrows were drawn low over his eyes.

"Uh, sorry," Vincent stammered. "It won't happen again."

What had gotten into him? He didn't even want to *look* at the art, much less touch it. He was here only because his mom had the wild idea that being with Uncle Leo would make Vincent want to start painting again. That definitely wasn't going to happen. If anything, being surrounded by art of this caliber made it clear he'd never been good at painting in the first place.

He waited for Uncle Leo to lecture him, but he just looked Vincent up and down, nodded, then turned and walked out of the room.

Vincent wanted to escape to his art-free room and

play video games, but first he needed to do what he'd come for. He hesitated, then set off after Uncle Leo. He found him in a small room with a large window through which he could see the girls still wandering the wildflower-strewn field. A boxy old computer sat on a small desk in one corner, two plush chairs in the other. Vincent felt his muscles relax at the sight of white walls without a single painting. Uncle Leo hunched over the only painting in the room, which lay flat on a large table with tools and brushes scattered across it.

Vincent stepped into the room. "Uncle Leo?"

His great-uncle looked up sharply, one eye strangely magnified by the jeweler's loupe attached to his glasses. He removed the glasses and tucked them into the pocket of his button-down shirt.

"What's on your mind, son?"

Vincent had planned only to ask about Georgia, but he realized he wanted to talk to Uncle Leo about something else. "I know that my mom only sent us here to get me interested in art again. It's not going to work."

"Of course not. You can't force something like that, and I don't intend to try." Uncle Leo pulled his glasses back out, adjusted them on his face, and leaned over the painting again as if dismissing Vincent from the room.

Was this reverse psychology? Feeling uncertain, Vincent began to back out of the room but stopped. He needed to get more information about his cousin. "Uh, Uncle Leo? Why didn't my mom want Georgia to be here?"

Uncle Leo sighed, a look of pain washing over his face. Vincent winced, wishing he hadn't been so blunt. The old man removed his glasses again and gestured for Vincent to sit in one of the two chairs. He sat in the other and rubbed the bridge of his nose.

"You caught that, huh? It's got nothing to do with Georgia and everything to do with our family." Uncle Leo paused, clearly choosing his next words carefully. "What's your mom told you? About the family, I mean."

Vincent shrugged. "Not much. I know she calls you sometimes. But she doesn't really talk about the rest of her family. I think maybe because of the fire."

His grandparents' house had caught fire, killing them and his mom's sister ten years ago. His mom never talked about it. All he knew was that no one had survived.

"The fire." Uncle Leo nodded. "A tragedy. So much great art lost."

Vincent frowned. "And people," he said sharply. "I think my grandparents and my aunt are more important than a bunch of art."

A look of discomfort crossed Uncle Leo's face, and his eyes grew glassy. Vincent instantly regretted his harshness.

"Mom said you were an art restorer," he said, trying to change the subject. "Why don't you work at a museum?"

Uncle Leo stroked his mustache and nodded as the tension dissipated. "I'm a conservator, actually. My job is to preserve the integrity of the art and the artist's original vision. I used to travel around a fair bit to different museums. But when you're the best, people come to you."

"So museums just mail you famous paintings to fix?"

"Courier. With lots of insurance."

Vincent didn't really know what a courier was, but he nodded anyway. "So . . . if it had nothing to do with Georgia, what were you and my mom whispering about?"

"Family secrets."

Vincent waited for him to elaborate, but instead, Uncle Leo stood and walked back to his table. Vincent rolled his eyes. Game over. He stood. "Thanks for letting us stay. We'll try not to bother you."

"Remember," Uncle Leo called after him, "don't touch the art!"

"Don't worry," Vincent said. He had no intention of getting any closer to the art than he had to.

He trudged up to his room, then lay on his bed, playing a retro *Zelda* game until long after dark, wishing he had a magic flute like Link to whisk him away to anywhere besides here.

Vincent woke to creaking floorboards. This dumb old house wasn't even going to let him sleep.

Quiet footfalls passed his room. A doorknob rattled, and hinges creaked. Probably one of the girls using the restroom. Vincent waited to hear footfalls returning to the girls' room a few minutes later, but no sounds came back down the hall. Was he imagining things? He'd never get back to sleep if he kept expecting another noise. He might as well check whether the hallway was empty. Vincent threw off his covers.

He stepped into the dark hallway, cringing as the floor creaked. The bathroom door stood open, but strangely, so did the door that had been locked earlier.

Vincent crept to the doorway and peeked in. The room was empty.

Well, empty of people, anyway. Faint moonlight through window blinds illuminated groups of angular objects that were draped in white sheets and covered most of the floor. He peeked under the nearest sheet to find stacks of framed paintings and cases that most likely held more paintings leaning upright against the wall. Vincent assumed the rest of the sheets hid more of the same. Maybe this was where Uncle Leo stored the paintings that were "couriered" to him by museums—probably why he kept this room locked.

But Vincent wasn't here to look at more art. Someone had walked past his door and into this room. The open door proved that. But where were they? He shivered, remembering Georgia's comment about the boogeyman. That was nonsense. Maybe he had dreamed the noise. Or maybe he was just feeling out of sorts sleeping in this weird house. But then . . . who had unlocked the door?

He fumbled for the light switch and flicked it on.

"Hello?" After navigating around the covered paintings, he peeked inside the closet, but it held only another sheet with more paintings hidden underneath.

Vincent turned to head back to bed but suddenly noticed an uncovered painting sitting in an open velvet-lined case. It hadn't been visible from the doorway. Otherwise he would have noticed it first thing.

The Starry Night. By Vincent van Gogh. The artist he was named after.

Could it be the real *Starry Night?*

A poster version used to hang over his bed at home, though now it was somewhere in the back of his closet. It was one of the most famous paintings in the world.

But that had to be in a museum somewhere, right? Vincent

crouched to take a closer look at the familiar painting. A clump of trees dominated the foreground in the shape of dark flames. A village nestled in the valley below, and blue hills rose in the distance. Candlelit windows seemed to flicker in small homes surrounding a white church with a steeple pointed like a spear toward the sky. That sky called to Vincent. The yellow crescent moon shining like the sun. The stars, whose glow radiated outward like ripples in water. And the swirling clouds, which made the whole painting feel alive with movement.

Vincent's skin tingled as the painting pulsed with energy. It tugged on him like a strong tide. He leaned in closer, and before he could realize what he was doing, he reached a trembling hand toward the painting, and . . .

The whole room tipped.

Vincent fell forward, spiraling, his body pulled and stretched. Then—*slam!*—he collided with cool, damp earth.

3

What just happened? One minute, he had been crouching next to the painting, and the next, it felt as if he had fallen into a churning ocean, been pulled under by a riptide, and then been spit out flat on his face in a dark grassy field. Thankfully, it was a fairly soft place to land.

Vincent pushed himself to his knees and looked up with a groan.

"What in the . . ." A brilliant sky swirled above him—the exact sky of *Starry Night*. Had he literally warped into it?

No way. This is a dream. It has to be.

He stood and brushed dirt off his face and arms, looking around. The landscape was exactly like the painting he'd stared at a thousand times when it hung as a print above his bed. Now van Gogh's characteristically thick brushstrokes surrounded him.

The towering cypress tree. The village scattered across the valley, candlelight streaming from each window. The tall steeple of the dark-windowed church. The swirling sky threw a kaleidoscope of light and shadow over everything. It was exactly like the painting, but it wasn't just a super-zoomed-in view. He was actually in *Starry Night*. But not a flat version. This world was three-dimensional and *real*. As if to confirm his thoughts, the cypress branches rustled, and a breeze brushed Vincent's cheek. And although he could see the individual brushstrokes on the ground where he'd landed, it hadn't felt at all like dried paint. The grass had been soft and damp, and Vincent's hands still felt grainy with dirt.

Suddenly he realized he wasn't alone.

"Georgia?"

His cousin sat just a few feet away, arms around her knees, staring at him with a relieved look on her face.

"For a minute, I thought you were . . . Anyway, you startled me," she said. Then her eyebrows scrunched together. "Wait—I didn't think you knew how."

"What?" He was confused enough without Georgia talking nonsense.

She stood and brushed grass off her too-short pajama

pants. They were the kind you buy as a set—they just weren't from the same set as her top. "I mean, you obviously aren't very good at it or you wouldn't have landed like that." She laughed, but then her eyes widened, as if she'd just realized something. "Was this your first time?"

"No, I get sucked into magical paintings all the time, because that totally makes sense," Vincent said. "What are you talking about?"

She cocked her head and stared at him. "You know . . . traveling."

Something in the way she said that word sent a shiver of recognition through him. Hadn't his mom and Uncle Leo been talking about traveling? Was this what she hadn't wanted him involved in?

He felt there might be no going back from the question he wanted to ask next. Like suddenly finding out you were color-blind and everyone had been seeing things you couldn't your whole life—and you never knew. "What's . . . traveling?"

Georgia grinned and threw her arms wide. "You just did it. Traveling is stepping into a painting. Getting to walk around in the mind of an artist."

Vincent's head spun as the sky continued to swirl in a mad dance above him. "Stepping into a painting like it's a real place?" This didn't make any sense, despite what his eyes were telling him. It was like someone insisting magic was real and he was a wizard. Which should have felt amazing, but instead, it made him nauseated.

"Well, falling in, in your case," Georgia corrected.

He pushed down his discomfort and asked another question. "Why is it called traveling? Do you go on vacations in paintings or something?"

Georgia's eyes sparkled. "Follow me." She turned and walked toward the edge of the painting.

As Vincent followed her, he noticed that this painted world didn't go on indefinitely. Instead, near where the edges of the real painting would have been, there was a blurry gray wall. When he turned his head back toward the sky and the town, the gray wall seemed to vanish. But when he looked back toward the edges, there it was again, like they were in a giant box.

Georgia continued to walk straight toward the gray wall. What did she want to show him? As if she'd read his mind, she turned to him, winked, and then stepped through the wall and vanished.

"Just when I thought this couldn't get any weirder . . ." Vincent shook his head. "And now I'm talking to myself."

He inched forward, hand outstretched, expecting

to feel a damp mist or maybe a solid wall. Instead, his hand disappeared. He yanked it back. It hadn't hurt, and his hand looked normal. If he wanted answers, he didn't have much choice but to follow, so he took a deep breath and stepped through the gray into darkness.

"Georgia? Where are you? Where are *we*?" He blinked rapidly, trying to get his eyes to adjust.

Georgia's laugh came from just in front of him. "Welcome to the Corridor! What do you think?"

The Corridor? Vincent's eyes began to adjust, and he noticed windows radiating soft light off to the right and left of what seemed like an endless hallway. The windows cast enough light for him to see Georgia but did nothing to illuminate the space they stood in. Everything was shrouded in blackness: above, below, and even the walls the windows were set in. Or maybe there were no walls and the glowing windows just hovered like portals. He turned in a slow circle and froze when he saw a glowing version of *Starry Night,* complete with the same frame he'd seen it in a few minutes ago, hanging in what seemed like mid-air.

"Did we just come out of that?" He looked at some of the nearest glowing windows more closely. Each one was a framed painting but backlit as if it were stained glass.

Georgia laughed again. "Do you like van Gogh?" she asked, ignoring his question.

Old Vincent would have said van Gogh was his favorite. He'd loved the vivid colors, the intense brushstrokes, the strong moods of van Gogh's paintings. But he'd left that all behind when he gave up art.

"I'm named after him." He hoped this answer would satisfy Georgia.

"Obviously," she said. "I asked if you *liked* him."

He shrugged. Being in *Starry Night* had been pretty cool. Amazing, really. But he wasn't ready to admit that. "I guess."

"The painting we were just in is *Starry Night* by Vincent van Gogh," she began.

Vincent rolled his eyes. "My mom's an art teacher. I know stuff—I'm just not into it." He didn't need an art lesson. He just wanted to know what was going on.

"So do you *know* any van Gogh paintings besides *Starry Night*?"

Vincent thought a moment. A van Gogh depicting a yellow field with crows flying above it had always fascinated him. "The one with the crows."

"*Wheatfield with Crows*?" Georgia arched an eyebrow. "That's a bit dark."

Vincent shrugged. It matched his mood about this whole bizarre situation.

"Okay." She motioned toward the left. "It's not too far. This way."

He followed Georgia down the Corridor as they passed a steady row of shining paintings on either side. Most of them Vincent had never seen before, but they all looked like van Gogh's style. Like *Starry Night,* each one seemed to glow from within. When he stopped to stare at a painting, it tugged at him like the tide, so he hurried to catch up.

Finally, Georgia stopped in front of one of them. "Here we are."

Vincent stared at the glowing version of *Wheatfield with Crows.* It pulsated, and the birds almost seemed to be moving. "Now what?"

"Just touch it."

Vincent's hand trembled as he reached out toward the painting and its magnetic tug. Just before his fingertips reached it, gravity shifted, and he was falling.

"Oof." Vincent hit the ground hard, knocking the air from his lungs. Mad flapping filled his ears as crows scattered, cawing angrily. Wind whistled past him and slapped wheat stalks against his face. The sky was dark and heavy. The air smelled of coming rain. He caught his breath and rose slowly.

"You have to work on your landings." Georgia stood

beside him, hands resting on her hips. The wind whipped her short red hair, making her look wild and sprite-like. She turned her face to the sky, brow furrowed. "Let's not stay too long."

Vincent turned back to the horizon. It was growing darker by the moment, and the crows, whose cries had been so loud moments ago, were vanishing into the distance. The painting was quickly growing ominous.

He shuddered. "Why? What could happen? It's just a painting, right?"

"Let's just say art isn't always safe."

He wasn't ready for this to turn into a nightmare. He looked around for an escape. Like *Starry Night,* this painting seemed to be enclosed in a giant box. They had entered facing the world of the painting, and on either side were the hazy gray walls. When he turned around, Vincent was surprised to find a shimmery wall mirroring the painted landscape like a reflection in a lake. A framed window hung in the middle of the wall, but it didn't show another painting or even the Corridor like he expected. It looked out onto somewhere else entirely.

"Where does that go?"

"A museum. But I think we've had enough adventure for your first time."

Georgia's tone was playful, but a museum sounded

like the opposite of an adventure to Vincent. He cringed at the thought of entering one. He glanced at the sky. It was darker now, and lightning flashed in the distance. Southern California didn't have big storms like this, and Vincent didn't want to be caught in the middle of this one. In fact, he wanted to be done with this whole Traveling business and go back to bed.

"How do we get back to the Corridor?"

"Left or right." Georgia pointed toward the edges of the painted world. "In any painting, left or right will get you to the Corridor."

She started to the left, and Vincent followed. As they made their way back through the darkened Corridor, Georgia chattered excitedly the whole time, but Vincent couldn't focus on her words. This was too much to take in. He'd come to Uncle Leo's hoping to avoid the art as much as possible. Now he'd been sucked into magical paintings and Corridors and who knew what else.

He almost bumped into Georgia when she stopped in front of *Starry Night*.

"Was *Wheatfield with Crows* what you expected?" she asked.

Vincent shook his head. "No. It was a lot more . . . powerful." Powerful like a massive wave—awe-inspiring but strong enough to pull you under.

"That's a good word for it." She reached out, touched *Starry Night,* and vanished.

He took one last look around and followed.

Vincent stumbled, hands catching grass before he face-planted. Clearly, he hadn't mastered landings. Not that it mattered, since he wouldn't be coming back here.

Georgia stretched out on her back, staring up at the swirling sky. Vincent rolled over next to her.

"Van Gogh felt closer to God through nature," she said. "That's why the sky is so alive but the church is dark."

Vincent had noticed the dark church before but never really thought about it. His family went to church only a few times a year, but sometimes, out in nature, like when he was staring at the Pacific Ocean with the wind whipping his hair, he had a similar experience. At times like those, God felt close but transcendent, like being enveloped in a cloud.

He hoped she didn't expect a response from him, and thankfully, she kept talking. "For me, it's art that does that—makes me feel closer to God, I mean. I think that's why I keep sneaking in here."

Vincent could kind of understand that. There was something about looking at *Starry Night* from the inside that made him feel as though his chest were opening up—in a good way. It was like recovering a sense of wonder he used to have about the world. He tried to remember whether art used to make him feel this way, but his mind only replayed the painful day he'd quit painting. He pushed down the memory.

They remained quiet for a while, mesmerized by the dark sky and swirling stars above until Vincent let out a big yawn.

"I'm going to stay awhile longer, but you can go back to bed if you're tired," Georgia said. Vincent stood and brushed himself off. He walked toward the window leading back to Uncle Leo's. "Just step while you're reaching this time," she called after him. "And we can meet tomorrow night after Lili falls asleep. There's a ton of things I want to show you."

Vincent ran a hand through his curly hair. She wasn't going to like this, but he had to tell her. "This was cool and all, but I'm not coming back."

Georgia shot up. "What do you mean? Why not?"

The last thing Vincent wanted to do was dredge up the worst day of his life, so he kept it simple. "Art's just not my thing."

"But it is!" Georgia flung her arms wide. "You wouldn't—couldn't—be here if you didn't have some connection to art."

Vincent shrugged. "Whatever." He didn't want to argue. He barely knew this girl, and he'd probably never see her again after this week.

Georgia turned away, arms wrapped around her middle. "Just don't tell Gramps that I can pick the lock, okay?" Her words were strained.

"Sure." Vincent felt bad, but he wasn't going to change his mind. He took a final look at the swirling sky. Maybe—probably—this had all been a dream. But even if it wasn't, this was the last time he'd see a painting from the inside. A heaviness settled over him. He heaved a sigh, then reached for the window.

Vincent woke up with his head pounding. The sound of clattering plates and Lili's excited chatter filtered through his door. He groaned and rolled over. He felt like he hadn't slept a wink.

Wait. He sat up. *Last night . . . That was just a dream, right?*

It had felt so real, but falling into paintings wasn't something that actually happened. This house must be getting to him. He couldn't even escape from art in his dreams.

Vincent rubbed his face as he walked toward the bathroom. He stopped, took a step back, and stared at the closed door. He tried the handle. Locked. He cringed, realizing he'd almost hoped that the door would swing open to reveal *Starry Night*.

Ridiculous. What was he even thinking? It had probably always been locked. Another junk room.

Vincent's head still ached when he went down for breakfast. Lili gave him a quick wave but continued chattering to Georgia, whose hair possibly looked wilder than it had yesterday.

"Morning, sleepyhead." Uncle Leo jerked the frying pan so that the pancake flipped in the air and landed on the other side. "Should be enough grub on the table for you. Don't know how much teenage boys eat nowadays."

"I'm just twelve, Uncle Leo."

"Humph."

Vincent rumpled Lili's hair and sat down across from Georgia. He tried to make eye contact with her as he loaded his plate with pancakes, but she stared at her plate, seeming intent on avoiding his gaze. That was weird, right? Maybe last night wasn't just a dream. . . . But no, it had to be.

Lili launched into a story about one of her friends from school, but Vincent couldn't focus. His dream kept nagging at him as he ate. It couldn't have been real, but he still couldn't shake it. Maybe he should just ask about the room. If Uncle Leo confirmed there was nothing important in there, it would prove last night was a dream and Vincent could get it out of his head.

"What's in the locked room upstairs, Uncle Leo?"

Georgia's head shot up, but Vincent couldn't read her expression.

Uncle Leo sat and speared a few pancakes onto his plate before answering. "More art, of course. Some of it I just don't got wall space for. Some of it's paintings I'm working on restoring for museums or private collectors. Only like to have one of those at a time in my studio. Otherwise I feel like they're all staring at me, demanding their turn."

Another room full of paintings. That didn't help him rule out last night as a dream.

"Why's it locked?" Lili asked. "I wanna see all the pictures!"

"Some of those paintings are worth more than you and I put together." Uncle Leo sipped his coffee and shot a glance at Vincent. "Well, that ain't really true. A person's worth more than a picture, but some of those pictures . . ." He let out a long whistle. "Let's just say the owners would have my hide if anything happened to them."

Vincent looked over to find Georgia staring at him, but she turned away quickly and popped up from the table.

"I'm going to throw some pots," she said. "Want to come, Lili?"

"Sure." Lili jumped out of her seat and raced after Georgia. "Come on, Vincent!"

"Maybe later." His head still hurt, and throwing

pots sounded loud. Uncle Leo didn't stop them, but he seemed pretty hands-off about anything besides his "don't touch the art" rule.

Uncle Leo stood and collected the plates. "I'll be in my studio. Knock if you need anything."

Vincent had been sure that Mom's plot to get him painting again involved Uncle Leo lecturing him about art or at least forcing him to watch the restoration process. But after their talk yesterday, it didn't seem like Uncle Leo cared how he spent his time.

"So it's okay if I just play video games all day?" he asked. "You're not planning to force me to do art?"

"Forcing you to *do art* sounds like a plan destined for failure." Uncle Leo stroked his mustache. "So no. I'm not going to force you to do anything. But video games on a day like this seems an awful waste."

Vincent's shoulders relaxed. He may have to spend the week surrounded by art, but at least he wouldn't have to worry about Uncle Leo pestering him. His headache even felt better.

The girls' laughter drew Vincent to an enclosed porch at the back of the house.

"Watch this, Vincent!" Lili sat behind a small round table with a lump of clay on top. As usual, Mr. Rumples was tucked snugly at her side. With a whirring noise, the tabletop began spinning. Lili mashed her hands against the clay, and its shape shifted with each movement: short and squat, tall and thin.

So this was the wheel. He felt stupid that he'd ever imagined Georgia was talking about a fairy-tale spinning wheel instead of a potter's wheel.

"Is pottery what all the cool homeschoolers do?" Vincent asked. Pottery definitely wouldn't be a cool-kid activity at his school.

Georgia raised an eyebrow. "Pottery is what *I* do. And *I* don't care about being cool. I think it's *more* important to do what you like and not worry about what other people think."

Vincent felt his ears flush with embarrassment. Her comment made him feel exposed, like she knew exactly what he'd given up to blend in and be cool. But she couldn't know what it was like to fail in front of everyone. She didn't hang out with other middle schoolers enough to know how mean they could be.

"You have to try this, Vincent." Lili giggled as she continued to dig her fingers into the spinning clay. "It's better than sandcastles."

When the wheel slowed to a stop, Lili cocked her head

at the misshapen lump in front of her. "That's not what I thought it would look like."

"Cheer up, kid," Georgia said. "It takes practice. Art isn't about being perfect. Want to save it or start over next time?"

Lili bounced in her seat. "Save it!"

Vincent leaned against the doorframe and watched as Georgia shimmied a wire under the clay, cutting it away from the square base attached to the wheel. Why would Georgia even suggest saving something that was so far from perfect? Mom always told Lili that whatever she made was beautiful. She had told Vincent the same thing. Lili was still young enough to think everything she made was a work of art, but Vincent had seen his parents dump most of it in the recycling bin. He hoped she'd just grow out of her love for making things like most kids did. That would be better than having to find out the hard way that all your parents' praise was a lie the way he had. His stomach knotted at the memory.

"It has to air-dry before we fire it in the kiln," Georgia said, placing Lili's creation on a board and sliding it onto a shelf alongside dozens of pots, vases, and mugs. Some of them looked pretty good, while others were just strange—though maybe that was on purpose. Had Georgia made all these herself?

Georgia took a wet rag and wiped down the wheel,

then looked up at Lili with a grin. "Now for the fun part. Follow me!"

She took off out the back door, and Lili ran after her, her trusty stuffed animal tucked under an elbow. Not willing to be left, Vincent trailed behind them.

The girls had run through knee-high grass to an open gate that led down a sloping path and were disappearing into a cluster of trees when Vincent made out the sound of running water.

"Lili, be careful!" Vincent called, breaking into a run. Lili wasn't a strong swimmer, and last summer at the beach, she had almost drowned. No way was he letting her get hurt day two of their parents being gone.

He skidded to a stop in relief when he saw the girls wading into a shallow bend of a river. The water came up only to Lili's shins, and he felt a little silly for panicking as he watched her trying to catch minnows in her hands.

"Is your brother always so determined not to have fun?" Georgia asked, giving him a look that was both amused and annoyed. What did she mean by "always"? She barely knew him. What did she have against him?

"Sometimes." Lili giggled and made another grab at the water. "The fishies are nibbling my toes! It tickles!"

"You can't catch them that way. I'll show you how next time." Georgia laughed as she splashed water on her arms and rubbed at the splotches of gray clay till they disappeared.

Vincent sat on a fallen tree. Georgia's comment reminded him of last night. Maybe he could get some clue from her without sounding like he was losing it.

"Did you sleep okay last night, Lili? The house is pretty creaky."

"Yup. Mr. Rumples kept me safe." She nodded toward her bunny, who lay on a patch of grass near the bank.

Vincent looked at Georgia. "How about you? You're not used to having a roommate. Did you sleep okay?"

She gave him a puzzled look. "Eventually."

Did she hesitate before answering, or was he just imagining things? He knew his next question was weird, but he needed to get rid of this nagging sensation about last night.

"Did you . . . did you go into the locked room? I thought I heard someone in there."

Georgia's expression went from puzzled to surprised.

"I want to go in that room!" Lili stopped grabbing for fish, her voice pleading.

"We can't go in there, remember?" Georgia replied. "And how could I? It's locked, silly!" She made a goofy face that brought new giggles from Lili.

Should he keep pressing? She hadn't actually answered his question, but that didn't mean it wasn't just a vivid dream. Maybe Georgia was acting weird because she acted weird in general. He decided to let it go.

"Do you always clean up here after using your wheel?" he asked.

"Usually. There's a hose behind the house, but this is more fun."

"I don't want Lili coming out here without me."

"Such a worrywart."

"I'm serious." Lili had a habit of wandering off and getting herself into trouble. Especially when Vincent was supposed to be watching her. Plus, Mom had specifically told him not to let Lili go to the river without him.

"Nothing's going to happen. I've got it under control." Georgia grinned and splashed water toward him.

Vincent dodged and frowned. "You have clay on your face."

She swiped a hand across her reddening cheek and turned her attention back to Lili.

A small green head moving in the water caught Vincent's attention. "Snake! Lili, watch out!"

He ran into the shallows to grab his sister. Of all the Texas snakes he'd read about, water moccasins were one of the scariest.

He lifted Lili from the water and carried her to shore, his shoes dragging in the shallows. When he turned back, Georgia was reaching for the green head.

"What are you doing?" Vincent yelled. Was she some kind of thrill seeker?

Her hands plunged into the water and scooped up . . . a frog.

"Watch out for the scary bullfrog!" Georgia said, laughing as she held it up.

Vincent ignored her. "It's time to get back to the house. I'll take you swimming later," he said to Lili as he set her down. Lili sighed, but she put on her sandals, picked up Mr. Rumples, and took Vincent's hand.

Even here, with no one to impress, Vincent couldn't manage to be cool. And now he'd probably ruined his favorite tennis shoes. He should have brought an extra pair.

They turned and headed toward the house, leaving Georgia behind, Vincent's shoes squelching with each step.

5

In the shade of the front porch, playing video games, Vincent could almost pretend he was back in California. But even video games got boring after a while, especially single-player games, which, without the internet, was all he had. After lunch, he'd left Lili playing alone in her room with Mr. Rumples and the other million toys she'd packed. Who knew where Georgia had disappeared to? Maybe he should go check on Lili.

He found Georgia alone in their room. Vincent cringed at the loud Hawaiian shirt she wore under her short overalls.

"Where's Lili?"

Georgia looked up from the book she'd been reading and glanced around the room. It was clear she hadn't even realized Lili wasn't there.

"How long has she been gone?" Vincent asked.

"I don't know, worrywart." She rolled her eyes. "She's probably just downstairs."

How could someone this frustrating be related to him? "I just came from downstairs, and sometimes she wanders off. What if she left the house?" Could Lili have hurt herself on Georgia's wheel? Gotten into Uncle Leo's studio? Wandered outside and gotten lost? Or . . .

"The river!" Vincent took off down the stairs. Georgia's footfalls came pounding after him, but it didn't matter. Lili was his sister, and he was the one who'd feel responsible if something happened to her.

"Lili!" he yelled as he yanked on his still-damp tennis shoes, burst out the back door, and sprinted toward the river.

It seemed to take twice as long to reach the river as it had this morning, and Vincent struggled to catch his breath as he looked along the riverbank. There was no sign of Lili. Or Mr. Rumples. Her shoes weren't here either, and Lili always took off her shoes before wading, because she loved the feel of the sand and rocks on her feet.

"I'm sorry." Georgia stood panting beside him. "I should have been watching her."

"Let's just find her," Vincent said.

They walked up and down the bank, calling her name and looking for footprints in the mud for another fifteen minutes.

"Could we have missed her at the house?" Georgia asked.

"Maybe?" They hadn't really taken time to look. He couldn't remember whether the bathroom door had been open or closed. She was probably back at the house, wondering where *they* were. He'd overreacted again, just like the episode with the bullfrog.

They trudged back toward the house.

"Sorry for freaking out," he said. Georgia may have called him a worrywart, but she had come to help him look. Maybe she wasn't so bad.

"It's okay. It must be nice to have a sister to worry about," Georgia responded.

"Yeah, some people think it's weird that we're so close since she's adopted," he said. "But she's still my sister." If anything, Vincent felt more protective of her, knowing she had once been without a family. She had been so scared when they first brought her home, like she thought they might disappear on her. He didn't want her to feel that way again.

"I kind of get that. My mom's from Mexico, and since I look like my dad, people never think we're related." She glanced at him. "I'm sure Lili's fine."

Vincent nodded, but his stomach still churned with worry.

Lili wasn't in the screened-in porch or the kitchen or anywhere they searched downstairs. Vincent took the stairs two at a time and checked the girls' room again. Empty. His room was empty too. The bathroom door stood open—also empty. But . . .

The door to the third bedroom was cracked open. Had it been that way before?

"Lili?" Vincent started toward the door, but Georgia tried to push past him, causing them to tumble through the doorway together.

The room was filled with white sheets draped over angular shapes.

No, no, no. This was impossible. He threw a sheet back to reveal paintings stacked against the wall. Vincent's head spun with déjà vu.

He threw back another sheet. More paintings.

He walked deeper into the room, and there it was. *Starry Night.*

It lay in its case, just like last night, beckoning to him.

But no, it *had* to have been a dream.

"Lili? Stop hiding, please." He could hear the desperate edge in his own voice.

"Vincent, calm down." Georgia gently placed a hand on his shoulder, but he shrugged it off.

"Calm down? We can't find Lili!" Vincent squeezed his eyes shut. "I thought this door was locked?"

"I couldn't remember if I put everything back where it was last night, but Gramps called me." Georgia shrugged apologetically. "I thought I'd locked it again, but even if she came in here, there's no way that Lili could go in *there*." She gestured at the painting.

"I thought it was a dream." Vincent's voice cracked. "Did we go . . . inside that painting?" He pointed at *Starry Night*.

Georgia sighed. "That explains why you were being so weird today. It wasn't a dream."

"But what . . . ? How . . . ?" If last night wasn't a dream . . . this was a nightmare.

"Our family can Travel through paintings," Georgia said slowly, like she could tell he was spooked. "It's hereditary. Your mom really didn't tell you any of this?"

She definitely had not. But a vague memory sparked inside Vincent. Before she was an art teacher, his mom had worked at a museum. He couldn't have been older than three or four. He remembered reaching out, touching a painting, and being transported to a strange world. He remembered his mom coming to get him. He had later written it off as a dream. Even though his mom bought him art supplies and books and constantly praised his artistic "gift," Vincent realized that was the last time he had ever been to an art museum. After that, his mom had begun teaching art history at the high school.

"But . . . that's impossible. Are you sure this house isn't just magic?" Vincent asked, but the argument felt hollow.

Georgia crossed her arms. "There's no such thing as magic. And what's impossible is for Lili to have Traveled. It's hereditary—you have to get the gene from your parents."

"We've checked everywhere else," he said. "What if you're wrong?" Lili could be lost in a painting and not know how to get out. Or worse, she could be wandering the Corridor. He shuddered at the memory of the ominous storm in *Wheatfield with Crows*. He knelt in front of the painting. Maybe he'd be able to see her if he looked close enough.

"Just stop." Georgia held up her hands in surrender. "You can't find her that way. Wait there, and I'll go check."

"Are you kidding?" As much as he didn't want to get involved in art, there was no way he was going to be left behind. "She's my sister. I'm coming with you."

Vincent stumbled and fell to his knees, disoriented and woozy. At least he hadn't face-planted like last night.

"You get used to it," Georgia said. "Like being on a boat."

This wasn't anything like getting your sea legs on a boat. They'd just warped into a painting like they were in some real-life video game. He looked up at the brilliant yellows and deep blues of the swirling night sky. He didn't think he'd ever get used to the wonder of actually being *in* a painting either. Maybe his friends back home would think art was pretty cool if they could experience it like this.

He suddenly remembered why they'd come in the first place.

"Lili!" he yelled. He'd expected to see her as soon as they stepped into the painting, but as he glanced around, she was nowhere in sight.

"I told you—there's no way she's in here."

"She has to be! We've looked everywhere else!"

Vincent turned away from the town to look behind them. A framed view of the room at Uncle Leo's hung at eye level like a photograph in the middle of a shimmery wall that reflected a muted version of the countryside.

"Could Lili have heard us talking from in here?" Sometimes Lili hid when their parents discussed things, even when it wasn't a real argument. Had she heard Vincent and Georgia talking and tried to hide?

"Only light passes through the window, not sound."

Where could Lili be? Vincent turned back to the painting and looked down the hill toward the village. His stomach knotted with worry. Or guilt. "Lili! Please don't hide!"

Maybe she was too far away to hear them. He looked at Georgia. "Where do we start? She could be anywhere."

"Well, the number of wheres inside a painting is generally pretty limited," she said. "You can only go forward into it. Left and right both lead to the Corridor, and the window behind us leads back home."

"What about all that space around the window?" Vincent waved his arm toward the shimmery landscape surrounding the view of the room in Uncle Leo's house.

Georgia marched past Vincent and slapped the air next to the window. It thudded dully, sending ripples through the view.

"There's nothing there. This is the artist's mind—or a projection of his mind that was created when he painted *Starry Night*, anyway. We can only go in the direction he could see clearly—into the painting. What's behind us doesn't really exist."

"What about the Corridor?" He didn't like the thought of Lili in there alone.

"*If* she's here," Georgia said, "it's very unlikely she'd have found the Corridor. People don't typically try to walk through walls. I guess she could have gone into the town. But I still don't think—"

"Oh no!" Vincent's gaze had shifted to the large cypress on the far left side of the painting.

Just past the base of the tree lay Mr. Rumples. Or more precisely, half of Mr. Rumples. His floppy head rested against the blurry gray wall at the edge of the painting.

"If Mr. Rumples is here, then so was Lili," Vincent said, running toward his sister's favorite toy. "Something must have happened to her if she's left half of it behind!" He grabbed Mr. Rumples by the ears. The rest of the stuffed rabbit materialized in Vincent's hand, nearly causing him to drop the toy.

"Hold on," Georgia began. "Something's not right."

Vincent ignored her and dove through the wall into blackness.

"Lili!" His voice echoed down the hallway, mocking

him. Vincent looked around frantically. Mom and Dad had trusted him to look out for her. She was only six. He'd been worried about rivers and rattlesnakes, not magic paintings that swallowed you whole. He spun around, but the hallway was just blackness dotted with windows of light. Lili was out there, scared and alone. She didn't even have Mr. Rumples.

"Vincent, listen to me," Georgia said as she entered the Corridor.

Vincent rounded on her. "You left the door open. You said she couldn't Travel, but she did. And now my sister could be in *any* of these paintings! How can we find her?"

"I'm not sure we can."

"What?" She couldn't mean that. Lili couldn't just be gone.

"Like you said, she takes that bunny everywhere. Would she ever willingly leave it behind?"

Vincent looked down at Mr. Rumples. He'd been clenching it so tightly the creature looked deformed. "She wouldn't leave him."

"Then I think she might have been taken."

"Taken? But you just said only our family could Travel. Who could take her?"

Georgia sighed. "I'm going to be in so much trouble, but it's time we talk to Gramps."

"But what about finding Lili?" He didn't see how Uncle Leo could help. Plus, lost or taken, they needed to look for Lili *now*.

"Trust me," Georgia said. "He can explain things better, and this is much bigger than we can handle on our own. We need his help."

Vincent didn't really trust her, but at this point, he didn't see another option.

6

Vincent and Georgia burst into Uncle Leo's studio without knocking.

"I thought I told y'all—" Uncle Leo began.

"Lili Traveled!" Georgia said, cutting him off. "We couldn't find her, and we looked everywhere, and somehow the door wasn't locked, and then she was gone, and—"

"Did you see her do it?" Uncle Leo interrupted. "She shouldn't have the gene. She's probably out in the field picking bluebonnets. And gosh darn it, Georgia, if I didn't tell you to stay out of that room and not get them involved."

Vincent held up Mr. Rumples. "She never leaves this anywhere. It was in the painting."

"Which painting?"

"*Starry Night*," Georgia said.

Vincent had expected Uncle Leo to run upstairs and charge into the painting. He had expected Uncle Leo to know exactly how to find Lili. Instead, he watched his great-uncle begin to pace back and forth, mumbling.

"Bad idea . . . Should have known . . . I promised her . . ."

This wasn't helping. Uncle Leo needed to pull it together.

"You have to get her back."

Uncle Leo paused and glanced over at Vincent. His eyes looked wild, like an animal caught in a trap. Vincent's body tensed. There was nothing scarier than a frightened grown-up.

"I haven't been able to Travel in nearly a decade," Uncle Leo said. "One day just"—he motioned with a hand—"poof."

"What? But Georgia said . . ." This really was a nightmare. He knew he shouldn't have trusted Georgia. Not only was the only adult in the house scared, but he also had no way to help them.

"She shouldn't have been able to Travel." Uncle Leo was mumbling to himself again.

"We need to find Lili!" Vincent's fear had turned to anger. "If you can't Travel, who else can?"

"My parents," Georgia said, "but . . . they're off-grid on a mission. Do you have a way to get ahold of them?"

Uncle Leo shook his head. "Not quickly enough to make a difference. If we could contact your mother, Vincent . . ." Uncle Leo trailed off. "But even then it's unlikely the cruise ship will have any way for her to Travel back here. There's no one else left."

Vincent pursed his lips. He couldn't just do nothing. "Well, I can Travel. If you can't help, then tell me how to find Lili!"

"What a confangled mess." Uncle Leo began pacing again. "I promised your parents not to get you involved."

"It's too late for that," Vincent said. "Lili is lost—or worse! Someone has to get her back."

"Gramps, do you think *they* took Lili?" Georgia asked. "Do they know you have *Starry Night*? Are they coming after us again?"

Vincent tensed at the edge of fear in her voice. "Who is *they*?" He watched as Uncle Leo shot Georgia a resigned glance. "What aren't you telling me?"

Uncle Leo sighed. "You'd better sit on down. I'll start from the beginning."

"Art is powerful. It has always had the power to draw people in," Uncle Leo began.

Vincent couldn't believe Uncle Leo wanted to give an art lecture at a time like this. From the sound of it, Lili hadn't just gone missing in a painting—she had been kidnapped. Yet here they were, talking about art.

But he listened as his great-uncle explained how artists expressed ideas about politics, society, human nature, and religion and that the best art expressed truth in a way that people needed to hear. That made it dangerous for those who sought power. Throughout history, people had stolen art—or destroyed it—to solidify their authority. Hitler, for instance. The British Empire. The Romans taking from the Greeks. Stealing masterpieces, stockpiling them, and even destroying art was all about power. Even in the modern world, protesters throw food at priceless paintings, and thieves sell their services to the highest bidder, the money going to fund terrorism and other nefarious activities.

Vincent grew impatient. "But what does stolen art have to do with finding Lili?"

Uncle Leo held up a hand. "I'm getting to that— I promise."

"Traveling is a great gift," Uncle Leo continued. "And because it's hereditary, it's also a rare one. Those of us who seek to do good with that gift call ourselves Restorationists."

Something about that word sent a thrill down Vincent's spine.

"But there are others," Uncle Leo said, "the Distortionists, who have twisted this gift and use it to steal art, create propaganda, and destabilize societies. They even have subtle ways of manipulating art. A painting altered from within can distort the artist's intentions. Art meant to bring joy will now bring unrest. Or produce hatred instead of empathy. In their hands, art becomes a means of propaganda instead of epiphany. These feelings seep into culture and politics. They create distrust and make people susceptible to misinformation. They spread in little ways and big, causing fear and hatred, suspicion and prejudice. It can go as far as leading to things like shootings. Acts of terrorism. Even—what is it?—ogres on the World Wide Web?"

"Trolls, Gramps," Georgia corrected. "As Restorationists, it's our job to find the stolen paintings and to fix what they tried to distort. We protect, recover, and restore art."

Vincent couldn't believe what he was hearing. "You're saying these Distortionists took Lili? Why can't you ask the Restorationists to help?"

"Like I said before, we're it," Uncle Leo replied, his voice sounding small for once. "About ten years ago, the Distortionists massacred most of the Restorationist families. They must have found some inside information. Me, Georgia's parents, and your mom are the only ones still alive."

When Uncle Leo didn't continue, Georgia picked up the story. "There used to be dozens of Restorationist families around the world. My mom is from a Restorationist family in Mexico, but there were Restorationists from Europe and Asia and Africa—all over. But . . . basically they're all dead, and we're in hiding. My parents are in the field, undercover, mainly trying to recover stolen art, especially since Gramps lost . . ." She glanced at Uncle Leo, who looked away. "Lost the ability to Travel.

"But honestly, we haven't seen much activity from the Distortionists in a long time," Georgia said. "Most of the stuff my parents end up helping Interpol with are just regular thefts. But they are the only other people who can Travel, so since Lili went missing in a painting . . ."

This had gone from bad to impossibly bad. If he understood everything Uncle Leo and Georgia had just told him, supervillains had taken his sister. "So who do we call? The FBI? What are we supposed to do?"

"The thing to do is wait for Georgia's parents to make contact," Uncle Leo said, staring hard at them. "They're the only ones equipped to attempt a rescue."

"But . . . how long will that be?"

"Not sure," Georgia said. "They only dropped me

off a day before you. They said they'd check back in a week."

"A week? No way." Vincent was on his feet. He started toward the door. "I promised to look out for her. I have to get her back *now*. If you can't help me, I'll find her on my own."

"Hold your horses," Uncle Leo said. "You can't just go after her—"

Vincent ran out of the studio and up the stairs. He couldn't believe he had trusted Georgia. Uncle Leo hadn't helped at all—instead, Vincent had gotten an art history lesson, and the only thing he had learned was that his sister was not just lost but in danger. He had no idea how to get Lili back, but he had to try.

But when he reached the doorway of the third bedroom, he stopped, frozen. What was he thinking? He didn't know what he was doing. He wasn't some trained Restorationist like Georgia. He didn't even like art anymore. He had no idea where to start looking for Lili, and if the Distortionists were as scary as Uncle Leo and Georgia described, he didn't even know what the dangers might be.

A hand gripped his shoulder, and he spun around.

"It's my fault she got lost," Georgia said. "If you're going after her, you have to take me as well."

He was still mad at her, but he knew he needed her help. "Fine."

"But we at least have to pack some supplies. And Gramps has some tools that can help us." Georgia gently steered him back downstairs.

He allowed himself to be led to the kitchen, where he slumped into a chair and watched as Georgia stuffed food into a doodle-covered backpack and then began rummaging through random drawers.

Uncle Leo walked into the kitchen, holding a leather satchel. "I can't stop you, and I won't try, but y'all need to do this the smart way. There's no sense in two untrained kids going up against heaven knows how many Distortionists."

He set the satchel on the table in front of Vincent and slid a weathered wooden box from it. "These are a Restorationist's tools. Normally you'd be getting your own set about your age, so it's only fitting you take my old one." Uncle Leo unlatched the box and swung back the lid to reveal a paint set.

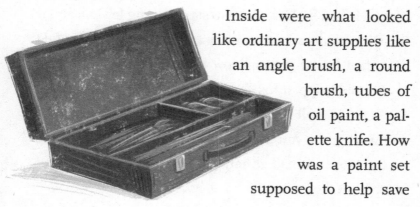

Inside were what looked like ordinary art supplies like an angle brush, a round brush, tubes of oil paint, a palette knife. How was a paint set supposed to help save

Lili? Where were the magic wands? The stones of power? Vincent thought they were dealing with real-life bad guys.

"I don't get it."

"Georgia can explain how to use these," Uncle Leo said, fingering the bristles of a fan brush. "And I'm sure your mom gave you some training, even if you didn't realize it at the time. See where Lili's trail leads, but then track down Georgia's parents. Georgia knows how to get to their safe houses, and y'all can at least leave a message for them. They'll know what to do."

Finding Georgia's parents made sense. Vincent doubted his mom had given him any training, unless training meant knowing the color wheel and how to mix paint. He didn't see how any of these tools would help Lili, and he certainly didn't feel confident that *he* could help Lili if these were the tools he needed to use. He hadn't held a paintbrush in more than a year. What was he supposed to do if he ran into one of these Distortionists?

Uncle Leo turned to leave but stopped in the doorway. "I know what it is to lose a sister." His lips quivered for a moment. Vincent wondered now whether the Distortionists had started the fire that killed his grandmother— Uncle Leo's sister—along with Vincent's grandfather and aunt. He shuddered. These were dangerous people.

"Y'all got a hitch in your giddy-up?" Uncle Leo's voice snapped Vincent back to the present. "Get a move on!"

He spun and hurried from the room, but not before Vincent noticed a tear start down his cheek.

"Was he crying?" Vincent shifted the bag awkwardly.

"I'm sure he misses his sister." Georgia stared at a ball of pink paracord before tossing it into her backpack. "But it's also hard for him not to be able to Travel anymore. Imagine you suddenly couldn't walk after having been able to fly. He's got to feel pretty powerless, especially right now."

Traveling into the paintings had been a magical experience—at least last night before he was worried about Lili. And for someone who obviously loved art as much as Uncle Leo, that must have been a difficult thing to lose.

"Why can't he Travel anymore? Is he too old?"

Georgia shrugged. "Maybe? He hasn't been able to Travel for as long as I can remember—he restores art by hand now, from the outside—but it's not like I have a ton of people to compare him to. The only other Travelers I know are my parents."

That sounded pretty lonely. Even though he didn't really understand this whole scary, magical world, Vincent thought it must stink to have this special ability and not be able to share it. Like having a secret identity but no one who really knows you. No wonder Georgia had been disappointed when he told her last night that he never wanted to Travel again. "Is it hard not being able to tell anyone about . . . all this?"

"Who would I tell?" Georgia pulled a flashlight from the drawer and placed it in the backpack. She sighed. "Once, I tried to tell one of my online friends. She just thought I was making up a cool role-playing story. That was the last time I tried."

Vincent knew the feeling of having a part of yourself you couldn't share. Something that would make you seem like a weirdo. Maybe they had more in common than he thought. She certainly wasn't the worst person to have on his side right now. Maybe they could really do this. They had to.

7

"First we need to find Lili's trail," Georgia said, tightening the straps on her backpack.

"And once you do, get yourselves to a safe house," Uncle Leo said firmly. "You can give me a call from there after you leave a note for your parents." He rested a hand on the frame of *Starry Night*, which sat propped in its case. "You know I can't leave the gateway open."

Georgia nodded. "Right. What's our way home, then?"

"The Rockwell. That leaves you plenty of options," Uncle Leo responded.

Trail? Gateway? Rockwell? It was like they were speaking a different language. "Am I supposed to understand what's going on?"

"Just stick together." Uncle Leo squeezed Vincent's shoulder and gave Georgia a hug. "Don't follow the trail more than an hour or so—probably won't last that long anyhow. And hightail it back here at the first sign of trouble," he added.

"Got it." Georgia gave another nod.

Vincent took a deep breath, trying to ready himself to Travel again, when Georgia gripped his arm with one hand and reached out for the painting with the other. Colors swirled as they were pulled into *Starry Night*. Vincent stumbled, but this time, Georgia kept hold of his arm, and he didn't fall, though that didn't stop the disorienting spinning sensation. He pressed his palms to the sides of his head and squeezed his eyes closed to make it stop. When he opened them, Georgia was already walking toward the gray wall at the edge of *Starry Night*. "Let's go," she called before stepping through.

Vincent hesitated. Even though they'd done it before, it was still creepy but also *way* cool to watch Georgia disappear. It was like finding a secret warp tunnel in his favorite video game. Except this was 100 percent real.

After stepping through the wall after her, Vincent blinked, waiting for his eyes to adjust. He turned a slow circle and jumped when Georgia seemed to materialize in front of him.

"Are you always this slow?" she asked, a hand on her hip.

Vincent rolled his eyes. "No, usually when I follow a guide through a magical world, I'm right on it. Sorry this isn't all normal for me like it is for you."

"Whatever. Come on."

Georgia strode purposefully down the dark hallway, but as they passed one painting after another, Vincent couldn't help looking. They each seemed to call out to him, beckoning him to visit the worlds waiting just beyond those glowing windows.

He'd never seen most of these paintings, but their style and color palette felt familiar.

"Are all of these van Gogh's?" he asked.

"Yeah. The Corridor is a link between all the paintings of a single artist," Georgia replied. "Every artist has a different Corridor linking all their work."

Vincent added this to his growing wiki of this crazy world he'd been thrust into.

"Are some of them not pitch black?" The paintings did nothing to illuminate the space, and it would be nice to at least see the floor he was standing on.

Georgia laughed. "No, they are all pitch black. The Corridor is kind of like an echo of an artist's mind. It can even reverberate with the artist's emotions."

The hair stood up on Vincent's arms. "Like van Gogh's haunting the hallways or something?"

"You have a wild imagination."

"Well, if *you* hadn't let my sister get lost in a painting, *I* wouldn't be needing to ask about all this weird stuff!"

"It's not weird, and stop blaming me! I said I was sorry."

"Well, *sorry* doesn't fix it!" Vincent yelled. He wasn't sure they'd ever find Lili this way.

The Corridor trembled.

"Shh!" Georgia held up her hand to silence him, but Vincent ignored her.

"You just like being in control!" he shouted. "You enjoy showing off that you know everything and I know nothing. Well, that's not my fault!"

The tremble had turned into a rumble that felt like an earthquake.

Georgia gripped his shoulder for support. "I told you the Corridor contains echoes of van Gogh's emotions. Your yelling is triggering a Disturbance!"

Vincent looked around frantically. He hadn't meant to yell, but in that moment, it was like someone else's emotions had washed over him.

The ground shook violently. "How do we get out of here?"

"This way." Georgia ran, dragging Vincent along the quaking Corridor. He barely registered the backlit paintings flashing by on either side of them until the ground shook harder, nearly knocking them over. Vincent steadied himself, then tugged on Georgia's arm to get her attention.

"Shouldn't we go into one of these?" he asked.

"I'm looking for something."

He could feel another deep rumble sweeping down the Corridor toward them. He was sure it would knock them over like a tidal wave. And if they fell in this blackness, Vincent worried they might fall forever.

"We have to get out of here now." Vincent pulled Georgia toward a painting with a huge vase of purple flowers against a yellow background. He reached out as the tremor swept by and grasped the painting's gilt frame.

Colors swirled and flew by—purple, green, yellow. His body squished, then stretched. This was more extreme than his previous Traveling experiences. He couldn't breathe. Then he was tumbling onto a wood floor, Georgia on top of him and his satchel wedged uncomfortably between him and the floor.

"Why on earth did you do that?" Georgia rolled off him, groaning.

Vincent's stomach was still churning, but the wooden floor felt cool as he rolled to his back. Wait. Where were they?

His eyes popped open. He'd expected to be in the painting, lying on an orange tablecloth beside a bunch of purple flowers. But this wasn't a painting at all. Instead, they were in a large, open room hung with paintings, dimly lit as though it were night. But it couldn't be nighttime yet. It had been late afternoon when they left Uncle Leo's, and they'd been in the Corridor only a few minutes. He sat up.

"Where are we?"

"My guess would be the Van Gogh Museum in Amsterdam." Georgia remained lying on the floor, her eyes closed. "And shush. The night guard might hear us if he hasn't already."

"Amsterdam!" Vincent hissed. "Where on earth is Amsterdam? And why didn't we just go into the painting like with *Wheatfield with Crows?*"

"Because you touched the frame, novice, instead of the painting. You should have just waited. Traveling straight through is not fun." She sat up, rubbing her head. "And Amsterdam is in the Netherlands."

Georgia was exasperating! A simple *thank you for saving us* would do. "It's better than being trapped inside an earthquake in van Gogh's mind."

"The Disturbance was just in the Corridor," Georgia said. "We could have waited it out in a painting. We'll have to go back in to find your sister's trail."

Georgia acted like he was supposed to understand all this, but he didn't even know *how* they were supposed to find Lili's trail. The Corridor was pitch black.

"Maybe you should actually explain things to me while we wait for that earthquake to stop."

"Sorry," Georgia said, sounding contrite. She climbed to her feet and held out a hand to help Vincent up. "I'm not trying to be a mysterious know-it-all. It's just complicated. It's like trying to explain breathing to a fish. I've been Traveling since I could crawl. It all just seems natural to me."

She started walking through the room, briefly checking the wall plaque beside each painting. Vincent followed until he spotted a camera in an upper corner of the room. "Don't we need to stay out of sight? What if we get caught here?"

Georgia continued going from plaque to plaque. "Night guards in museums are notoriously underpaid. It's probably some college student doing homework instead of watching the cameras. Besides, when I find what I'm looking for, we'll be out of here in a second."

"Can't we go back the way we came in?"

"We don't want to enter too near that Disturbance. I'm looking for the right date. The right location. If we enter too far, we might miss what we're looking for."

She clearly couldn't *not* be a mysterious know-it-all. "What *are* we looking for?"

"The Luminescence."

"What's the . . . What was the word?" He couldn't keep up with all this new terminology. Traveling. Corridor. Restorationist. Now *Lumi*-something.

"Luminescence," Georgia said. "It's like a slight additional glow—well, maybe not an actual glow, but there's a small difference about the light surrounding a painting that's been Traveled through recently. It's like Hansel and Gretel's breadcrumbs. The Luminescence *is* your sister's trail."

"Hansel and Gretel's breadcrumbs get eaten." If their ability to track Lili was as reliable as breadcrumbs, they were doomed.

"Right. The Luminescence won't last forever, which is why we need to get back to the Corridor." Georgia stuck her head around the corner before stepping into the next room. This time, Vincent followed.

"Then shouldn't we—"

"Shush, or I'll never find what I'm looking for," Georgia said. "Go keep a lookout for the guard."

She didn't have to be so bossy, but at least that sounded like a good idea for once.

Vincent stepped through a doorway onto a large wrap-around balcony with a waist-high parapet. The balcony surrounded a multistory open space about the width of a basketball court. He kept away from the balcony's edge and walked a little way along a wall that was papered over with a large image of Vincent and Theodore van Gogh's gravestones. Creepy. Just beyond, the wall gave way to floor-to-ceiling windows, their shades glowing from the city lights beyond.

Vincent sat on a bench, his back to the windows. There was no point in continuing around the balcony when this was a perfectly good lookout. He could clearly see the two stairways in the near left corner and the two sets of glass double doors leading to rooms across from where he sat.

He had been sitting for only a minute when he noticed movement in one of the rooms diagonally across the balcony from him. He ducked under the parapet to avoid being seen and started to crawl back toward Georgia to warn her.

"No! Mommy wouldn't like it. I want Mommy!"

The voice sounded exactly like his sister's.

"Lili?" Vincent peeked over the parapet.

A dark-haired boy dressed in black was hushing a

little girl about Lili's size. He held her hand and was trying to draw her through the glass double doors into a room across the balcony. When she turned, Vincent shot up from his hiding place. "Lili!"

"Vincent!" She broke free and ran, but the boy was faster. He grabbed her and cast a frantic glance across the balcony. When their eyes met, Vincent realized the boy couldn't be much older than he was. What was going on?

Lili screamed, and two taller figures in black with ski masks emerged from the doorway. One of them scooped Lili up and put her over his shoulder.

Vincent had been frozen in panic, but as Lili disappeared through the doorway, he broke into a run. He forgot about the guard. He forgot about how dangerous the Distortionists were. All he knew was that he had found his sister and this might be his only chance to get her back.

He raced down one end of the balcony glancing across at the glass doors on the opposite side that Lili's kidnappers had carried her through. He couldn't lose her again.

He was rounding the corner near the stairways when his arm yanked back. Georgia held him in a tight grip.

"Let go!" he yelled, trying to shake her off. "They have Lili!"

"Eh! Stoppen!"

A stocky blond man was trotting up the stairway from the ground floor while fumbling for something on his belt.

"Quick!" Georgia pulled Vincent back toward the stairway that led up to the next floor.

"But . . ." He wrested his arm from her grip and glanced back at the doors Lili had disappeared through.

"She's already gone! Come on!" Georgia was halfway up the stairs, and the guard had nearly reached him.

Vincent hesitated a moment longer, then darted after his cousin. The guard's boots pounded not far behind them, and an out-of-breath voice shouted at them in whatever language they spoke in Amsterdam. The guard had been trying to pull something off his belt earlier. Museum guards weren't armed, were they? Vincent hadn't been to a museum in years—and certainly not in Amsterdam. Who knew how things worked in a museum halfway across the world?

Georgia probably did. Georgia and Uncle Leo, who spoke only in secret code and had yet to tell him anything useful.

Instead of another balcony, this stairway ended at a door, which Georgia flung open and raced through.

Vincent followed, narrowly avoiding being thwacked by Georgia's backpack as she swung around to grab his arm and yank him through one large room into another. She kept a tight grip on him, even when they stopped in front of a row of small canvases. She ducked her head to scan the plaques under each.

Boots clomped in the room behind them. More yelling in the language Vincent didn't understand. They were running out of time.

"This'll have to do." Georgia reached for one of the paintings, and in a swirl of dark colors, the museum disappeared.

8

Vincent shook off Georgia's grip. He couldn't believe she'd stopped him from saving Lili!

"Why did you pull me away? She was right there!"

Georgia's expression soured from relief to anger. "So you want to barge in on a group of Distortionists, who probably have weapons, while they are in the middle of a robbery? And let's not forget the museum guard. You think that's going to end well? It's bad enough that you yelled her name. Now they know we're coming for her."

"Coming for her? They're long gone."

A large puff of smoke set Vincent coughing as it billowed around him in painted swirls. He hadn't looked at the painting before Georgia pulled them in, but he definitely hadn't expected to find himself standing toe to toe with Vincent van Gogh himself, though anything below the man's chest was a bit hazy. Had this painting expanded to let them in? This self-portrait didn't have the flamboyant colors of van Gogh's more famous paintings. Also, the man standing before him was dignified—definitely not what Vincent would have expected. The only reason he recognized his namesake was van Gogh's characteristic red hair and, well, they'd come from his museum. Van Gogh puffed on his pipe again and muttered something Vincent couldn't understand.

"Uh, sorry." Vincent sidestepped toward the edge of the painting and into the Corridor. Georgia followed.

"Okay, Miss Know-It-All. Now what?" Vincent asked.

"Shhh!" Georgia hissed. She looked up and down the Corridor. "We don't know where they came out," she whispered. "They could still be in the Corridor."

That didn't seem like a bad thing. Vincent wanted to rescue Lili as soon as possible. But before he could say anything, Georgia gave his chest a hard poke. "What a place to blow our cover," she said. "To have the whole stinking Van Gogh Museum off-limits when the only trail we have leads through van Gogh . . . Now it'll be swarming with cops for days!" She tugged her short hair.

Vincent crossed his arms. "You're acting like this is my fault."

Georgia spun and glared at him. "It *is* your fault," she

whisper-yelled. "You are supposed to let me lead, but you keep . . . doing things!"

Doing things? It wasn't his fault she'd never explained the proper way to enter a painting. And who cared when that mistake had led them directly to Lili? She couldn't expect him to sit helpless when Lili was right there.

"Well, you haven't done a great job at leading. Besides, it's my sister who is missing."

"And you think you can find her on your own? Let me know how that works out for you." Georgia turned and stalked off down the Corridor.

Vincent clenched his jaw. Georgia leading hadn't gotten them anywhere so far, and her failure to lock the door was the reason his sister was missing in the first place. Maybe he *would* be better off trying to find Lili on his own. What had Georgia said to look for? Illumination? He would find Lili and then take her somewhere. Anywhere. As long as it was in the real world. He could call his grandparents back in California. They could help them get somewhere safe. Forget about going back to Uncle Leo's. His mom's family was nuts.

Vincent walked in the opposite direction, gripping the strap of Uncle Leo's satchel. What was he even supposed to do with this? He walked slowly, examining each painting, though not quite sure what he was looking for.

They all had the same backlit glow, each a window into van Gogh's vision of the world, but none of them had any extra "glowiness" to stand out from the others. How was he supposed to find this Luminous-whatever? If only Georgia would just explain things to him beforehand instead of blaming him afterward. At least he was trying to do *something*.

Vincent let out a long breath, then continued down the Corridor. He had to pay attention if he wanted to find this trail.

As he walked farther, the style of the paintings shifted. Instead of the brilliant blues, yellows, and greens, these were filled with grays and muddy browns. Many were dark and dreary. Mom had shown him some of these paintings in one of her art history books. They were van Gogh's earlier works, before he moved to France. They matched Vincent's current mood: depressed.

Van Gogh must have hundreds of paintings, maybe thousands. Searching for Lili this way was hopeless. How would he find the special glow that told him where she'd gone before it faded? How long did he even have until this new trail disappeared? Yet another detail Georgia had forgotten to tell him. And even if he found the glow, he knew Georgia had been right about one thing—he couldn't expect to stop a group of supervillains and rescue his sister by himself. He'd probably just get kid-napped too.

His fingernails dug into his palms, and he closed his eyes and forced himself to take a deep breath. He'd worry about that after he found the trail. He had to keep looking.

Vincent opened his eyes, and one painting seemed to sparkle ahead of him. He hurried forward, heart racing. He studied the painting, which featured two water-wheels in front of a ramshackle building. An old wooden fence stood in the foreground, separating a small bit of grass from a muddy river.

Vincent looked at the paintings on either side of this one, then turned back to study it again. There was defi-nitely a different kind of glow around this one. It wasn't just the painting that was lit up, but a faint aura shim-mered around it, like when he found a special item in a video game. This had to be the Illumiscense or whatever Georgia had been talking about.

Vincent wiped his palms on his pants. This was it. He may not get another chance. He had to be ready to snatch Lili and run. They could head back to the mu-seum. He'd rather they got arrested by that guard than kidnapped.

He wondered whether he should go back and try to

get Georgia's help. No, so far, she had made things only worse. It was all up to him.

He took a deep breath, remembered to avoid the frame, and entered the painting.

Vincent landed in frigid water that rushed over his feet, soaking his shoes—again. At least he had landed on his feet and not face-first in the river. He sloshed out of the water and onto the thin, grassy patch of land and held on to the rickety fence to keep his balance. The waterwheels creaked as they churned, and the river burbled as it flowed past him. His landings might be better, but he was still surprised that a painting could feel so real.

Real . . . but empty.

No Lili. No kidnappers. Maybe he'd been wrong about the Luminosity he'd seen. It had been faint, after all. Maybe he'd wanted to find it so badly that he'd imagined it.

Vincent looked up at the framed window to see where this painting led. He could see a room crowded with people, several of whom wore uniforms.

He stepped closer to get a better view. They were police officers! And one was interviewing the guard who had chased them through the Van Gogh Museum! The guard gestured animatedly, seeming to indicate heights and other physical details.

Vincent couldn't hear him, but he guessed the guard was describing him and Georgia. But why this room? Vincent didn't recognize it as one they'd been in. Had the guard also seen the boy and the two hooded figures that took Lili? Maybe he'd even caught them. Maybe Lili was safe.

An officer shifted, and Vincent realized what made this room the focus of the investigation.

One section of wall—where a painting definitely should have been—was empty.

9

A sudden shove from behind sent Vincent stumbling forward, nearly dumping him into the river.

Vincent swung around, arms raised to defend himself, but it was just his cousin.

"You are such an idiot! Why did you run off?" Georgia tried to shove him again, but Vincent shuffled sideways and ended up shin deep in the water.

"I—"

"What was your big plan, huh? Get kidnapped along with your sister? Or get lost in a foreign country where you don't speak the language?" Georgia's face was almost as red as her hair. Her eyes sparked, and tears gathered in the corners.

"You told me to get lost." Vincent held his hands up in mock surrender, although he was surprised at how relieved he felt to not have to actually do this alone. But he wasn't going to let her know that. "I would have worked it out."

"No." Georgia shook her head, the tears streaming down her face. "There's a reason Restorationists work in teams. This is dangerous. You have no idea what you're up against."

Vincent laced his hands behind his head and blew out slowly. "You're right. I have no idea. My parents have hidden this world from me my whole life. All I know is my sister is missing, and when I tried to follow the Illuminati like you said—"

"Luminescence."

"Sure. I'm trying to say it led me back to the museum we just escaped from."

Georgia swiped the tears from her cheeks and peered through the window.

"That explains why they were Traveling through van Gogh. They must have run into Lili on their way. Stealing art is what they do. Or one of the things they do. Stealing kids is the weird part. At least, as far as I know. We've been hiding from the Distortionists so long that I guess I don't know what to expect."

"Did you see the robbers?" Vincent asked. "One of them wasn't any older than us."

Georgia's eyebrows drew together. "That seems weird."

They watched the cops trickle out of the room, leaving the guard staring at the blank space left by the stolen painting.

"So I'm pretty sure the night guard gave those cops our descriptions," Vincent said. "They probably think we stole it."

Georgia chuckled. "Great. I'm going to be grounded for life. But"—a smile spread across her face—"this is actually really good."

Vincent narrowed his eyes. Georgia was back to not making sense. "How is being grounded for life good?"

"Not that. The fact that those goons were just here with Lili. The trail will be fresh. We really have a shot at finding her. Much better than before when the only clue we had was *Starry Night*."

Vincent's breath caught. She had no idea how much he'd needed to hear that.

Georgia reached into her backpack and pulled out two granola bars. "Want one?"

He shook his head. "Shouldn't we be following the trail now?"

"This is actually a pretty good place to hide for a bit. It already had Luminescence, so that masks our trail in case *they* are looking for *us*." She bit into her granola bar and looked around. "And it seems pretty stable. . . . Oh."

That didn't sound good. Vincent followed Georgia's gaze. "What?"

"The waterwheel on the right—the bigger one. Look."

Vincent watched the interconnected wheels turn. The paddles of the larger one were pushed clockwise by the river, then connected with the smaller wheel to rotate it. It seemed to be working, so he didn't know what he was looking for. But then something blood red on one of the paddles caught his eye. He squinted and realized it was a symbol he recognized.

"Is that a swastika?" Vincent cringed. "That's horrible! Did van Gogh hide swastikas in his art?"

"No, he lived way before World War II," Georgia said. "That's the work of the Distortionists. Nazis aren't the only face of evil, but their symbols are an easy way to create a Distortion."

These really were the bad guys. "Can people looking at the painting see that? Like, wouldn't someone at the museum be able to tell the painting had been tampered with?"

"Not necessarily. Distortions are often imperceptible." Georgia walked along the fence to get a closer look. "Most people wouldn't even notice the subtle change they feel when looking at a Distorted painting. It's obvious when you're *in* the painting, but only a trained art conservator could tell something was wrong from the outside."

"Is that what Uncle Leo does now that he can't Travel?" Vincent pictured his great-uncle bending over a painting on his worktable.

"Yeah, he's the only Restorer left, but even with his skills as a conservator, he can't fix everything. It's easier to restore a painting from within." Georgia removed a small leather satchel from her backpack. It looked just like the one Vincent was carrying. "We'll just have to fix this one."

"We can't do that," Vincent said. "We have to find my sister."

"We will, but we need to do this first. This is an important part of being a Restorationist."

"I'm *not* a Restorationist," Vincent muttered, but Georgia was already climbing over the rickety fence. He sighed and followed. If they had to stay clear of the Corridor, he might as well see how Georgia planned to get rid of the swastika.

They edged along a narrow wooden walkway to where the waterwheels met. The wheels whooshed by, seeming a lot faster and more dangerous now that they were close.

Georgia pulled an art palette and some paints from her leather satchel. She squirted brown, yellow, and white paint from various tubes. Vincent watched her mix the colors with the flat edge of a palette knife, a tool his mom had taught him how to use.

Some artists even used a palette knife instead of brushes for painting. He remembered holding one and wondering why it was called a knife when it looked more like a tiny metal spatula. Could Georgia really fix this with paint?

"So how does this work? Do all Restorationists know how to restore paintings?" Vincent asked. Yet another reason he'd never be one.

"We all have different gifts," Georgia said, squinting up at the waterwheel. "Gramps said that most Restorationists would pursue careers that helped them move in the art world: curators, docents, appraisers, Interpol agents, conservators. During World War II, when the Nazis stole and stockpiled massive amounts of art, Restorationists spearheaded the Monuments Men's effort to recover it. Along with our ability to Travel, we each have a special skill set—a Gift—that helps us in those jobs. But we all learn the basics."

The basics. Was that what Mom had been teaching him when they used to paint? But why if she never intended to show him this world?

Georgia looked back and forth between her palette and the waterwheel. Vincent thought she needed more red ocher if she wanted to match the color. Not that he'd admit knowing that.

"You literally just fix it with paint?"

"Did you expect carpentry?" Georgia squirted a dab of red ocher, then blended again. Maybe she did know what she was doing. "The Restorationist has many tools, and paint is the most versatile. I'm not much of a painter, but thankfully, van Gogh's brushstrokes are pretty chunky, so if I think of it like sculpting, it should be a piece of cake. We'd be in trouble if it were someone with finer brushwork like Vermeer.

"Here's where it gets tricky," she said, watching the wheel's constant motion. "You're going to have to give me a boost so I don't get stuck between the wheels."

The wheel's paddles raced by, clacking together where they met. Was she serious? This wasn't a video game. Getting hit with one of those boards could do some serious damage. "Maybe you should just let your parents know so they can fix it later."

"Boost." Georgia scooped paint onto the palette knife, tossed the wooden palette on top of her backpack, and stood waiting.

With a sigh, Vincent laced his fingers together and squatted with his back to the wheels. Georgia stuck the tool between her teeth, then placed one foot in his hands, her hands gripping his shoulders.

"On twee," she said through clenched teeth. "Un, two, twee."

Vincent pushed upward, and Georgia caught a spoke of the rising wheel. It wobbled a bit under her weight but continued to turn, albeit more slowly. She clung to the wheel's rim with her right hand, wrapping her legs around it. Taking the tool in her left hand, she mimicked van Gogh's thick strokes, covering the offensive symbol. When the wheel passed its zenith, Georgia's weight pulled it swiftly toward the water as she hung on upside down. There was no way she could jump off in time.

"Georgia!" Vincent yelled as she went under. He knelt on the platform, scanning the water to find her.

But as the wheel inched upward again, Georgia was still clinging to it, drenched and grinning. She reached for Vincent's outstretched arm and swung back onto the dock.

"That—was—awesome!" she said, panting.

Vincent heaved a sigh of relief, but his mouth twitched

into a matching grin. "Yeah, it kind of was. I guess you do this kind of thing a lot?"

Georgia's smile faded. "No—I mean . . . Actually, my Gift is Navigation. This stuff is better for a Restorer like Gramps. Besides, I'm mainly a sculptor. Detailed brushstrokes are not my specialty, so hopefully we don't encounter any more Distortions."

She seemed suddenly uncomfortable. Did she wish she were a Restorer like Uncle Leo instead of a Navigator? Fixing Distortions seemed a lot more important

than reading maps. Vincent hadn't meant to hurt her feelings, so he changed the subject.

"So how does sculpting fit into being a Restorationist?"

"It doesn't." Georgia finished stowing her supplies and zipped her backpack.

"Then why spend so much time doing it?" For someone who seemed all about being a Restorationist, that seemed weird.

Georgia stared down into the flowing water, and then she said, "Why make art?"

Vincent felt gut punched. "I don't." Not anymore.

"I mean, why does anyone make art?" she said. "What use is it? What does it do?"

Vincent didn't like having a conversation about art turned back on him. He shrugged.

"Art expresses beauty and truth," Georgia said. "It's a gift. It's meant to be experienced and interacted with, not used. That's what's so gross about what the Distortionists do. They *use* art instead of making it or even enjoying it. They turn art into propaganda."

Vincent stared out at the river. He'd never thought much about the purpose of art. Georgia called it a gift. It used to feel that way, but that was something Vincent didn't think he could get back.

He let out a long sigh. That was enough thinking about art. "So can we go find Lili's trail and get a message to your parents now?"

Georgia bit her lip. "Things got a little more complicated when you tried to chase down her kidnappers in the museum. They know we're coming, which means they'll be swapping out gateways—unframing or covering paintings—just like Gramps did. So if we find the trail . . ."

"You mean this could be our one shot." Vincent bit his lip. He had no idea how this world worked or what he was doing. He wasn't some trained Restorationist hero. Even with Georgia's help . . .

"You found the Luminescence without any help. I fixed the Distortion," Georgia said. "I know we didn't get off to the best start, but we can do this if we stick together. A real mission."

More like real danger. But wasn't hiding from danger what made his mom keep this world from him in the first place? He was done hiding. "I can't let them have Lili. I have to do this."

Georgia grinned. "Then let's go!"

10

Glowing portals lined the Corridor, stretching as far as Vincent could see. And Lili could be on the other side of any of them. Their mission—if that's what it was—suddenly seemed impossible again.

"Where do we start?" he asked.

"Did you know van Gogh painted almost a thousand paintings, most of them in the last two years of his life?"

"Is that supposed to make me feel better?" Vincent rubbed his hand over his face. A thousand paintings! They'd be more likely to discover an Easter egg in a video game than find Lili's trail. Vincent was a good gamer, but it was impossible to locate those hidden bonuses without a hint. And there was no insider website or You-Tube walk-through of the Corridor to help them out. "We should have followed them right away."

"We were just in *Water Mill at Gennep*, painted in

1884, which means we're in an early section of the Corridor," Georgia said, ignoring his objection. "But they picked up your sister in *Starry Night,* one of van Gogh's later works painted in 1889. That means they must have passed by it on their way here, so their exit point has to be somewhere beyond *Starry Night.*"

"How do you know all that?" She'd just rattled all that off as easily as his mom, who had a master's degree in art history.

"I'm a Navigator. Come on. It's at least a mile's walk. Unless . . ."

Vincent waited, but Georgia seemed lost in thought. "Unless what?"

"You know your mom was a Navigator before . . ." Georgia bit her lip and glanced at Vincent.

"My mom?"

For the first time, it hit Vincent that his mom had really been part of this world, not just in on the secret. He imagined her Traveling through paintings, stopping bad guys from stealing or destroying art, and navigating her way through museums and Corridors like Georgia. Suddenly Mom seemed like a different person. Why had she walked away from all this?

"My parents talk about her sometimes," Georgia continued. "'The good old days,' they say. Your mom and her sister used to work as a team. Your mom was the

Navigator, and your aunt was a Tracker or something. She could sense if someone else was in a painting anywhere along an artist's Corridor, maybe even find old trails."

"That would be handy right now," Vincent said.

"That's what I'm thinking!" Georgia grinned like she'd been handed a new toy. "Every Restorationist has a Gift, and sometimes they're hereditary. You might take after your aunt. After all, you *did* lead us to the Van Gogh Museum, and you found the Luminescence. Maybe that was *your* Gift showing!"

Vincent threw his hands up in protest. "I don't have a Gift. I'm not even a Restorationist. I just want to find my sister."

"You can Travel, and you're part of this family. That makes you a Restorationist. Come on. Just try," Georgia coaxed. "That would be an amazing Gift—"

"Fine." He'd try. Not that it would do any good. "What do I do?"

"I guess just close your eyes and, you know, reach out with your mind or something."

Vincent sighed but closed his eyes. He might as well get this over with.

Lili, where are you? He pictured his sister, trying to remember her as he last saw her—hair down, purple T-shirt—but nothing magical or extraordinary happened. Not that he'd expected it to. *He* wasn't magical or extraordinary. He suppressed a twinge of disappointment and opened his eyes.

"I can't do it."

"Maybe you just have to try harder," Georgia said. "What about—"

"Stop!" Vincent cut her off. He'd had enough. He wasn't special. He wasn't a Restorationist, and he never would be. "I don't do art, and I don't have any magical skills. It's probably just a fluke that I can Travel at all— just like it's a fluke that Lili could. I didn't ask for any of this!"

Georgia held up her hands. "Okay, okay, no need to bite my head off. It's not always easy to find your Gift."

Vincent's stomach churned. Georgia didn't know him. A huge part of him just wanted to get out of here and leave this world behind for good, even though another part wished his mom hadn't hidden all this from him. Maybe he could have still loved art and even had a Gift if she had shown him sooner. But right now, he was here only to find his sister. And so far, he hadn't been of much use.

"Let's just find Lili, okay?"

"Right." Georgia nodded. "Like I said, it's a long walk."

She started down the Corridor, but Vincent hesitated. Despite Georgia's confidence in their direction, something didn't add up. Why would the thieves walk all that way when they could jump through any painting? As he turned in a slow circle, trying to fit the pieces together, a twinkle caught his eye.

"Can you see that?"

"What?" Georgia's voice echoed from the opposite direction.

"The light down there." Vincent tilted his head. He'd just seen it a moment, so maybe it was his imagination. But there it was again, similar to when he'd found the Luminescence but weaker, maybe farther away. "It's kind of . . . shimmery."

Georgia shuffled up beside Vincent and squinted into the darkness. "That's weird."

"What's weird?"

"Unless they took a shortcut."

"That didn't answer my question."

But Georgia was already striding down the Corridor, so Vincent followed, hoping she knew what she was doing.

"This is not good." Georgia stared at a detailed sketch of a river lined with bare trees and buildings in the distance, the Luminescence surrounding it obvious now that they stood in front of it.

"You mean we can't Travel through it since it's not a painting?"

"What? No. If it's in here, we can Travel into it. It's not good, because *this* piece of art is at the Met."

The Met? It took Vincent a moment to register that Georgia was talking about the Metropolitan Museum of Art in New York and not the Mets baseball team.

"Right. So we don't want to risk getting caught in another museum."

Georgia raised an eyebrow at him. "No. The only reason *we* almost got caught is because *you* chased down a gang of Distortionists. The issue is this piece is in storage."

Vincent threw his hands into the air. How was he supposed to work with Georgia if all she did was treat him like a little kid and make statements that were supposedly obvious but made no sense?

"Look, I'm not a mind reader. *Why* is it bad that it's at the Met in storage?"

"Artwork in storage isn't just left sitting out," Georgia said, pacing in a tight circle. "The fact they Traveled through it means either their hideout is in the Met, one of the world's most important art museums, really bad, or they have someone on the inside who works at the Met to leave it out for them, also bad."

Georgia was making him nervous.

She stopped pacing suddenly. "We need to figure out the time."

Vincent slid his phone from his pocket. "That's weird." He tapped the screen. "There isn't a time."

"Of course not, Einstein. You're not in a real place. You have to be in a place to have a time."

"You're the one who asked what time it is!"

"I meant in Texas. Never mind. I can do the math in my head. If we left around five, it's maybe six-thirty." Georgia cocked her head. "That's seven-thirty in New York, which means the Met will be closed. It could work."

"So how do we not almost get caught by a guard this time?"

"A storage room shouldn't be a big deal. The museum is closed, so no visitors. And the storage rooms are locked, so no guards."

"How could you be sure it's in storage anyway?"

Georgia tapped the side of her head. "Navigator."

"Isn't that just like maps and directions?"

She held her chin up. "A Restorationist Navigator knows museum layouts, art collections, which paintings are on display, which are on loan, and which are in storage." Maybe she wasn't jealous of Uncle Leo's skill after all.

They entered the drawing and then, after checking through the window, proceeded to the storage room.

Vincent turned in a slow circle as he took in the large, vacant room with its rows of shelving. Georgia used Vincent's phone to make a quick call to Uncle Leo, reassuring him that they were okay and still following the trail.

She didn't mention the run-in at the museum or their new, more dangerous plan.

"I don't think this is their base," Vincent said when she was done. He pointed to the activated alarm sensor on the doorframe. "Unless they know the code."

Georgia nodded. "But they did use it as a shortcut to another painting. Look."

Vincent followed Georgia's gaze to a table. It was a larger, fancier version of Uncle Leo's restoration table, complete with neatly organized tools. Another piece of art by van Gogh lay in its center.

"*Corridor in the Asylum.*" Georgia shuddered. "Not where I would have chosen to go. But it will lead us to the section of the Corridor with his later paintings. It's a smart shortcut."

Vincent leaned over the painting. He remembered it from his mom's art books. It had given him nightmares when he was little. "It's so weird how it looks cheerful and creepy at the same time."

"It's the yellow," Georgia said. "Yellow is meant to be happy. It's like van Gogh is always trying to cheer himself up. But that hallway looks endless." She gave another shudder before turning to Vincent. "We should be careful. It might be a trap."

"Paintings can have traps?" Apparently one more thing he didn't know to be worried about. Besides *Wheatfield with Crows,* none of the paintings they had Traveled through had seemed dangerous.

"No, but the Distortionists might have left one." She pointed to the lone figure in the painting. Van Gogh had painted a man, who looked like he was about to walk through one of the many doors down the long asylum hallway. He was far down the hallway, more a suggestion of a man than a detailed figure. "This guy. Is he a guard? An inmate? He creeps me out. They might have tampered with him."

"You just fixed a waterwheel while it was spinning! And he's way down the hallway. We'll be in and out in no time."

"We have to be smart," Georgia said. She held out a hand. "Open your satchel. Mine's scratched."

"Your satchel's scratched?"

"No, I need the . . . Just open it."

Vincent unslung the satchel from his shoulder and pulled out the dark wooden box. He placed it on the table and swung the hinged lid open to reveal the paint set. Who knew how these tools worked in the Restorationist world, but they looked ordinary to Vincent.

Georgia whistled. "This set is nicer than my mom's. You'd better take good care of it." She picked a small black velvet pouch from one corner of the box and slipped its contents into her hand. It looked like a super-compact telescope, similar to the one attached to Uncle Leo's glasses when he was working.

"This is a monocle," Georgia said, fitting it to her eye. She bent over the painting, holding the monocle centimeters above it. "It should help me spot most Distortions, but . . . I forgot how much these bother my eyes." She straightened and held out the monocle. "Why don't you take a look?"

Vincent started. "What?" Was Georgia faking? This felt like another Gift-finding test. "I'm telling you, I don't have any magical skill."

"Just take a look." She sounded exasperated. "It really does hurt my eyes."

"Fine." Vincent took the monocle, held it to his eye, and bent over the painting. The eyepiece magnified van Gogh's broad brushstrokes into sweeping lines. The yellow walls seemed to seep down toward the burgundy floor.

He focused in on the man. Vincent had flipped through Mom's van Gogh coffee-table book enough times to know something was off. He may have stopped caring about art, but he remembered how van Gogh painted human figures from a distance with featureless faces.

But this one had a face.

And it was the kind of face van Gogh never would have created.

The face had an evil grin.

And it was staring right at Vincent.

11

Vincent staggered back, clutching the monocle in his fist.

"Careful!" Georgia pried his hand open and snatched the monocle. She gave it a quick inspection and gingerly slid it back into its velvet case. "These are super expensive. I got in big trouble when I scratched mine." She slipped the velvet pouch back into the wooden case and closed the lid. "What did you see?"

"Hypothetically, what would happen if someone painted an evil face on a person in a painting?"

"I knew it." Georgia rummaged through the items on the table, then moved on to searching the storage room's shelves.

"What are you looking for?"

"Turpentine."

"You can't use turpentine on a van Gogh!" Vincent

was surprised at how much that horrified him. Artists—and maybe conservators like Uncle Leo—used turpentine to remove paint. But if Georgia wasn't careful, she might permanently damage the painting.

"It's okay. It would just remove the fresh paint. But I don't see any. We'll have to do this the hard way." She flung her backpack onto the table and dug through it. She held up a tool that looked like what the dentist used to clean his teeth, except the handle was wooden and, instead of coming to a point, this one ended in a flat, arched edge.

Vincent flinched. What was she planning to do with that? "I've never seen that in a painter's kit before."

"It's actually a ribbon tool for sculpting. I've watched Gramps use something like this loads of times," Georgia said with a shrug. "It should work the same."

That made Vincent even less confident in her competence. This might be a worse idea than the turpentine. "He's a trained conservator!"

"We can't leave him like this." She waved the tool at the painting. "It's bad enough that it's a Distortion, but they've basically created a little zombie guard to patrol the painting and keep us from getting through."

Vincent shivered. The only zombies he wanted to encounter were in *Minecraft*.

"Hand me the monocle," Georgia said. Vincent

reluctantly pulled the eyepiece back out of the case and handed it to her. She hunched over the painting, ribbon tool in one hand and monocle in the other. Her hand shook as it inched closer to the figure. Vincent held his breath.

She suddenly straightened, letting the tool clatter onto the table. "It's too risky." Vincent sighed in relief while Georgia paced, running fingers through her already-messy hair. "It would be different if we were on the inside, but this isn't my specialty, and if I damage the painting, we might not be able to Travel through it at all. Plus, 'first, do no harm' and all that."

"Like the oath that doctors take?" Vincent said.

"And Restorationists. I can't risk damaging a van Gogh. I can't."

At least she'd come to her senses. But they still needed to get through it to find Lili. "So now what?"

Georgia stopped pacing. "We go through quickly. If we land on our feet and run for the Corridor, he shouldn't be able to reach us. He's way down the hall."

"And if that doesn't work?" Vincent asked. He had yet to perfect his landing.

She held up her tool. "I'll try to fix it from within."

"What about damaging the painting?"

"It's harder to damage from inside. It's riskier for us but less risky for the painting."

"Like with the waterwheel?"

"Right."

Vincent sighed. He never would have guessed that he'd risk his life to not harm a painting. Wait—how risky was this bit?

"How dangerous is it in there for us anyway? Is it like in a dream where you always wake up before you die?"

"If you die in a painting"—Georgia stared hard at him—"you die."

Vincent swallowed. "And if you damage the painting trying to fix it from the outside, we can't Travel through it and . . ."

"We may never find Lili."

Vincent nodded. "Which way do we run—right or left?"

Corridor in the Asylum was one seemingly endless hallway with a long succession of doorways on either side. A small set of steps led to a door on the painting's front right corner, possibly blocking the exit to the Corridor, so the cousins had decided to run to the left upon entry.

But the moment Vincent stepped into the painting, he landed unevenly—his right foot ended up on the stairway and his left on the tiled floor. It was hard enough to keep his balance Traveling into a painting with flat ground, but uneven ground was a level up. He reached for Georgia to steady himself but tripped, caught her backpack, and sent them both sprawling deeper into the hallway. He glanced up anxiously, but instead of coming toward them, the man was disappearing through one of the many doorways.

Georgia shoved him off. Vincent rolled off his satchel and lay on the cool tile floor in relief.

"That wasn't so bad."

He glanced at Georgia. She had risen to a crouch, and her eyes were wide and frantic, looking at something behind him, at the front of the painting. Had someone followed them in? Vincent scrambled to his feet and turned. Walking down the last of the stairs Vincent had tripped on was the creepy man. Before they could react, he stood before them, blocking all exits to the Corridor. His eyes were black blobs of paint, his eyebrows arched menacingly, and a sinister grin hung sloppily on the left side of his face. He stuck out like a glitch in a video game, very obviously not what the creator intended.

"Run!" Georgia grabbed his arm and yanked him down the hallway, deeper into the painting.

Vincent glanced back, but instead of chasing them, the man stepped back onto the stairway.

"We're going the wrong way!" Vincent tried to turn around, but Georgia pulled him on. "The Corridor is back that way."

"This is a labyrinth," Georgia said, pulling Vincent toward a doorway.

"What are you doing?" He shook free of her grip. "Is it even safe to go through these doors? Where do they go? How are we going to find our way back out?"

Before she could respond, Creepy Guy stepped out of another doorway on their right. It was like he had just warped from the front of the painting.

"Run!" Georgia dove through the door, but Vincent didn't follow. Instead, he ran farther down the hallway, satchel thumping against his side.

He skidded to a stop when Georgia popped out of a door ahead of him. "See? Labyrinth. Normal rules don't apply here. You've got to trust me." She gripped Vincent's arm and glanced around cautiously. "My parents take me to M. C. Escher's art sometimes to train. You can't get lost because you always end up in the same place."

Vincent remembered checking out a book of Escher's mind-bending drawings from the library once. Several

of them showed impossible buildings that connected in weird ways. He couldn't imagine how disorienting it would be to be inside one.

Movement to Vincent's left caught his eye. He turned to see the Distorted man appearing from a door a few feet away.

Georgia pulled Vincent back through the door she had just come through. This time, they came out near the front of the painting.

"Let's get out of here." Vincent tried to move toward the Corridor, but Georgia's fingers dug into his arm.

"Wait," she protested. "I don't think we should leave him like this."

"Uh, yeah, we should."

The man appeared in a doorway near them, and Vincent tugged Georgia through another door. Now they were halfway down the hall. "What's going to happen when he catches us?"

"Nothing good," she admitted. "But things might be worse if this painting is rehung without being restored."

"What could possibly be worse than us being caught by Creepy Guy?"

Georgia didn't have time to answer since the man appeared near them again.

Wherever they dodged, van Gogh's Distorted character

seemed to follow. And he always emerged from a doorway just out of arm's reach.

"I have an idea," Vincent said after their twentieth doorway. "Can you be ready to fix him?"

"Uh, sure?" Georgia looked at her ribbon tool, as if she hadn't realized it was still clutched in her hand.

"Then stay here." Vincent swung her to face the doorway they had just exited. He took a deep breath and then dodged through the door beside her. He kept running, barreling straight forward through the next one.

Vincent kept going through one doorway after the next. He hoped he wasn't wrong. One of these doorways had to be right. He just hoped he wouldn't be too late.

After dashing through his sixth, Vincent emerged directly behind the painted man, who loomed over a terrified Georgia. Vincent flung his arms around the man, creating a human straitjacket. The man tried to free his pinned arms, but Vincent gripped his own wrists to tighten his hold.

"Quick! I can't hold him long!" For someone made of paint, this dude was strong.

Georgia raised the ribbon tool, and Vincent could hear it scrape against the man's skin. With each scrape, the man relaxed in Vincent's grip. He soon stopped struggling and stood still while Georgia removed the rest of the Distorted face.

Finally, Georgia let out a huge sigh. "Now who's the one withholding information?" She smirked at Vincent.

"A thank-you would do," Vincent said as he released the man. They watched him trudge down the hall. Before disappearing through a door, he turned his head toward them and gave them a nod.

Vincent never thought he'd be so relieved to see a man with no face.

Back in the Corridor, Vincent and Georgia examined painting after painting, looking for the next breadcrumb in their search. Surrounded by the bright yellows and deep blues of van Gogh's later works, Vincent couldn't help feeling a ray of hope.

Until he realized Georgia was muttering to herself.

"What?"

"Huh? Oh . . . it's just that most of these paintings belong to museums."

"Isn't most of his stuff in museums?"

"Yeah . . . but the Distortionist hideout isn't likely to

be in a museum. Sure, they might have special access, like at the Met, but they couldn't really have a whole base in a museum. And I don't think they would have booby-trapped that painting if we weren't really close to finding their hideout."

"Couldn't they just steal a painting and use that?"

"But I haven't heard of any recent thefts."

He started to ask another question when Georgia turned on him, her mouth open. "That's it!"

"What's it?"

"Come on. We're headed the wrong direction." Georgia ran back along the Corridor.

Vincent hurried to catch up. "Can you stop being so cryptic and just explain things clearly for once? Wrong direction for what?"

"I should have thought of it before, but your question made me realize that it didn't have to be a *recently* stolen painting. There's a van Gogh that was stolen in 1989, *Landscape in the Neighbourhood of Saint-Rémy*. I've only seen a black-and-white photo, but I'm sure I'd recognize it."

Vincent shook his head and chuckled. "You realize having every painting in the world memorized is not normal, right?"

"That'd be absurd. No one could memorize *every* painting."

Vincent gave *Corridor in the Asylum* a wide berth as they passed by again. Luminescence clearly surrounded the painting. Soon another painting with the same distinct glow came into view.

"This is it!" Georgia stood before *Landscape in the Neighbourhood of Saint-Rémy*, her head tilted. "Hmm . . . I'd always imagined the colors differently."

Vincent took in the painting. Its focal point was a white house with a dark roof standing in the midst of a yellow field. A thick swath of hilly reddish-brown road made its way from the foreground toward the house. Small trees or bushes dotted the landscape near the house. In the background, a white mountain range—or maybe they were clouds—stood out against a dark blue sky.

"It's beautiful." There was so much reverence in her tone. "It doesn't seem right that something beautiful should lead to somewhere evil."

Vincent remained silent. His whole world had turned upside down in the last few hours. Just yesterday, he had wanted nothing to do with art. He knew he could never create something remotely as good as the painting before him. It was painful to admit, but he had come to accept it. Now he wondered if he could open himself to art again. From the moment he landed beneath the swirling sky of *Starry Night,* the desire to create had been stirring in him again. Could he stay involved in this new world once they'd rescued Lili? He wasn't sure if he wanted that, if he was ready for it. He alternated between wanting to confront his parents about hiding all of it from him and just forgetting the whole thing. But none of it would matter if they couldn't find Lili. He needed to focus on the search—even in this world, art was just a distraction from what really mattered.

"You said they might close the way—unframe it like Uncle Leo did," Vincent said, breaking the silence. "How can we tell?"

"If it were closed, the painting would be dim, almost invisible compared to the glowing ones around it. We could still enter the painting, but we wouldn't be able to Travel to or even see a window to wherever the painting is. Framing a painting is like opening a gateway—connecting the artist's world, where we are, with the outside world."

That would explain why the paintings hung in Uncle Leo's house didn't have frames. Though it didn't explain why he'd been drawn so strongly toward one of them. It was the same way he'd felt before Traveling into *Starry Night.* "So you can't Travel into an unframed painting unless you're in the Corridor?"

"Well . . . maybe? But it would take a lot more concentration," Georgia said. "I've never been able to do it. And even if you did get in, you definitely couldn't Travel back out the same way."

"Should we be worried about more booby traps?"

Georgia examined the painting closely. "I don't see anything to worry about. They probably don't expect us to have gotten this far. It should be safe to enter the painting. We can scope out the room and make our plans there."

Vincent nodded. "Okay, let's go."

They grasped hands, reached forward, and stepped into the painting.

Only, someone else was already there.

12

A boy stood on the painted path as if waiting for someone. Not a boy made of paint. A real boy. And Vincent recognized him.

"He's one of the museum thieves!" Vincent called to Georgia. He shifted to block the exit window. "He's a lookout!"

The boy feinted to the right toward the Corridor, and Georgia took off in the same direction. But Vincent caught a slight smirk on the boy's face and was ready when the thief switched directions to dash toward him. Vincent planted his feet and braced himself. The boy barreled into him, and they fell onto the path, red dirt flying everywhere. The boy writhed underneath him, trying to get free, but Vincent was bigger.

"Who are you?" Georgia stood over them, hands on hips, clearly frustrated at being outsmarted.

The boy stopped struggling and craned his neck toward Georgia. "You two are here for the girl? Lili? She told me about you. Vincent, right? I can take you to her."

"I don't trust him." Vincent adjusted his position and held the boy's wrists in a tight grip. "Do you have some rope so we can tie him up?"

"What's your name?" Georgia asked while she dug in her backpack.

"Ravi," the boy said. "When is the rest of your crew coming to rescue us?"

"Our crew?" Vincent asked, then instantly wished he hadn't. This kid was probably trying to mine them for information. "And what do you mean 'rescue *us*'? You're the one who kidnapped my sister!"

"Wasn't me," Ravi protested. "The Lady dropped her with us on her way to a meeting. I was trying to take care of your sister." His eyes flitted from Vincent to Georgia before widening. "You two aren't here to rescue her alone, are you?"

Vincent's jaw clenched. He wasn't sure what made him more upset, that he'd just blown their cover or that this kid was claiming he was taking care of Lili when he was the one who had kept her from breaking away at the museum.

"Hold out your arms," Georgia said. She wrapped a length of pink paracord around Ravi's wrists.

"Make sure it's tight," Vincent said.

Georgia raised an eyebrow at him. "I think I know how to tie a knot." She moved to secure Ravi's ankles next.

Once Georgia finished the last knot, Vincent shoved off the boy's back.

Georgia dusted red dirt off her knees and walked over to peer out the exit window. Vincent joined her. It opened to a nondescript medium-sized room. Light from an open door revealed a long table at its center surrounded by black office chairs. He didn't see any other paintings—framed or otherwise.

"It looks like one of the conference rooms at my dad's office," Vincent said. He was surprised that the enemy lair would look so . . . well, normal.

"They might be like the mob and have companies as fronts for their operations," Georgia said. She nodded back toward Ravi. "We could use his help."

Vincent shook his head. "No way. Too risky."

"Is going in blind better? We can at least get some intel."

Vincent sighed, and they turned to face the boy.

"Ravi," Georgia said, "can you help us find Lili?"

Ravi nodded. "Sure thing. Just untie me, and I'll take you to her."

"Not a chance," Vincent said. He didn't think Georgia

was falling for the kid's routine, but he was going to make where he stood very clear, just in case.

Ravi searched their eyes before sagging in defeat. "Okay, um . . . when you leave that room, you'll turn that way." He jerked his head to the right.

Vincent raised an eyebrow. "Right?"

"Sure, right. When the hall ends, go that way." This time, Ravi jerked his head to the left. Vincent's eyebrows rose higher. "Follow that hall around a corner. Door at the end is where they keep the Wanderers."

These directions sounded iffy at best. "Are you sure we can tru—"

"What are Wanderers?" Georgia interrupted.

"You know," Ravi replied, "all the kids the Lady has fished out of paintings. Like your sister."

Georgia gave Vincent a look and led him a few yards away. "This makes no sense," she whispered.

"I know. It's clear he's giving us fake directions—"

"No. That last thing he said. Wanderers? It makes no sense that regular kids—non-Restorationist, non-Distortionist kids—would be wandering into paintings. I mean, it's weird enough that Lili could Travel without being biologically related to someone who can, but a whole group of kids wandering around paintings? It's just not possible."

Georgia's mind was so wrapped up in all this

Restorationist stuff, but all Vincent wanted was to rescue Lili. "I don't get why that's such a big deal."

"Traveling is hereditary," Georgia said. "Random people don't just wander into paintings. One kid is an aberration. But lots of kids Traveling? It goes against everything I know."

Vincent ran his hand through his hair. Georgia had been his guide to this crazy world, but they were both just kids. "Maybe there's stuff you don't know yet."

"Maybe, but my parents and Gramps made sure I knew all the rules." Georgia stared into the distance. "Unless they didn't know that could happen."

"Or they hid it on purpose—lied—like my parents did." He loved his parents, but he also knew that this wasn't the first time they'd been dishonest with him. His mom had lied about his artistic skill when she must have known he wasn't that good. They'd even lied to keep him from visiting museums, planning family vacations and doctor's appointments that conflicted with school field trips. They may have thought they were protecting him, but they'd wrecked his trust to do it.

And now this whole situation. It made Vincent's stomach churn. If his parents had just trusted him with the truth, he could have protected Lili. Watched her better. Something. He shouldn't have to be rescuing her.

Georgia bit her lip. "We can only do our best with

what we know." She looked back at Ravi. "We don't even know if he's telling the truth."

Vincent took a deep breath and gave a determined nod. "Then let's go find out."

He'd been sure Ravi was sending them into a trap. But as Vincent and Georgia tiptoed out of the room and followed the directions, no one jumped out at them, no alarms sounded. It was completely quiet as they passed what looked like classrooms, a gym, and a cafeteria.

They now stood in front of a closed door marked STORAGE. Georgia looked at Vincent and shrugged. He tried to turn the handle, but the door was locked.

"Now what?"

Georgia rummaged through her backpack and removed a small zippered pouch from which she produced what looked like two thick needles attached to metal handles. "I've got this."

He watched as she stuck the tip of one into the lock and held it there while she inserted the second above and wiggled it up and down.

"Is that a lock-picking set?" She was definitely still weird, but his cousin was proving to be kind of cool.

"As if my parents would let me buy that. These are ceramics needles." Georgia held her head near the lock. "Now, shh. I have to be able to hear."

There was a slight click, and Georgia stepped back.

Vincent slowly twisted the knob and opened the door a crack to peek inside.

The room was no storage closet. It was basically another long hallway, dimly lit. Plexiglass walls revealed rows of small cells, about twenty total. The walls between the cells were also plexiglass, revealing a desk and a cot in each. Most of the cots held sleeping kids.

Vincent stepped out of the way to let Georgia get a look. "I think Ravi was telling the truth."

Georgia peeked inside, then stepped back. "They *can't* all be Travelers. They must be Distortionist kids."

"Then we should probably be worried about whether they'll attack us when we walk through that door."

"Be ready to run," Georgia said. She swung the door fully open and stepped through.

The cells each had a single overhead light that dimly illuminated the space. Vincent and Georgia could just make out the occupants. The cells on the right side of the room seemed to hold all girls. The ones on the left, boys. Whoever these kids were, they couldn't be Distortionists, could they? Most of them were very young. Few seemed as old as Vincent and Georgia. One little girl in pigtails barely looked four or five. All the kids were dressed in plain, matching gray pj's.

"It's like a prison," Georgia whispered.

Some of the kids were awake. One paged through a

book at her desk. Another paced back and forth in the small space. He was the first to notice the intruders. His eyes widened, and he rushed to his door and banged a palm on the glass, yelling to be let out, which woke a few others.

Georgia shrank back at the sudden attention, but Vincent didn't care. Because there she was.

Lili was in one of the last fishbowl-like cells. She sat on her cot, knees hugged to her chest, crying. Vincent ran forward and pressed his hands to her door. "Lili!"

Her head shot up. "Vincent!" She jumped from her cot.

Vincent expected the door to be locked, but when he tried the handle, it flew open.

Banging and shouts from other kids rose around them, but Vincent was focused only on his sister. He bent down, and Lili threw her arms around his neck.

"I knew you'd come!"

"Are you okay?" he asked. "Did they hurt you?"

"No," Lili said, "but things have been really weird."

Georgia tapped Vincent's shoulder. "We should get out of here before—"

The hall door swung open, cutting her off.

A lanky teenage boy with an irritated expression stepped in. Behind him came Ravi. So much for Georgia's knot-tying skills.

Ravi pointed at them.

Vincent looked around for an escape and noticed another door, closer to this end of the room. "Run!" He grabbed Lili's hand and dragged her toward it.

"Wait," Lili said. "That's the—"

"No time." Vincent scooped her up and sprinted the rest of the way.

Georgia reached the door first and swung it open.

It was only a bathroom.

Vincent turned back, hoping they could maybe make it past the teenager and Ravi. But they had already closed in.

They were trapped.

The older boy pointed a black bar at them. Electricity sparked from its tip.

Vincent wasn't willing to give up. They had found Lili against all odds, and he was going to get her out.

Still holding his sister, Vincent tried to dodge around the electric stick, but it connected with his shoulder. Pain pulsed through his arm.

His body went rigid. Then he was falling.

13

Vincent woke to a banging that matched the pounding in his head. He opened his eyes to find himself lying on the floor in one of the fishbowl rooms.

This couldn't be happening.

"Time to wake!" a German-accented voice called out, followed by more banging. From his place on the floor, he could make out a teenage girl with two tight braids making her way down the line of cells, banging on each of the doors.

"Ladies first," Tight Braids yelled.

Buzz-click.

The cell doors on the opposite side of the hall opened, and girls trickled out.

Vincent sat up quickly, and his vision spun. He stood and groped toward his cell door. Except his remained locked. He jiggled the handle as he watched girls shuffle toward the bathroom. When he picked out Georgia and Lili among them, he banged on the glass.

"You! Stop that!" Tight Braids stood before his cell, scowling. She had a black stick in her hand. Vincent stepped back and sat on his cot, remembering his earlier encounter with one of those. Tight Braids turned to the girls and prodded stragglers into the bathroom. Georgia and Lili cast helpless expressions his way as they passed.

He looked toward the cells on his side of the room and realized none of the boys had been released. Some were sitting up in their cots, but a few were still lying down.

How had this happened?

Twice he'd found Lili, and twice he'd failed to rescue her. And now he and Georgia were prisoners too. If it hadn't been for that boy Ravi. He'd grabbed Lili in the museum. And then he lied and said he wanted to help them but instead led a guard straight to them.

Vincent noticed something on the floor of his cell. His phone! He looked around to make sure no one was watching and then bent to pick it up. All he had to do was call Uncle Leo. He didn't know exactly where they were, but Uncle Leo could probably figure out based on the painting they'd Traveled through. He scooted to face the corner of his cell, thankful it was closest to the bathroom and had glass walls on only two sides. But when he turned his phone over, he found the screen was black. A crack spread across it like a spiderweb. However many times he tried to turn it on, it didn't light up. Great. Now he'd be grounded. If he ever got out of here.

There was no rescue coming. They'd never left a message for Georgia's parents. And Uncle Leo couldn't Travel. Vincent didn't know how long he'd been unconscious, but whatever trail they'd left in the Corridor was likely long gone. They had to find their own way out, or they'd be trapped in these fishbowl cells forever.

But even if he could get the girls and run, where to? Would they have unframed the painting they entered through or moved it to another room? He needed more information, and he wouldn't get that trapped in this cell. He'd just have to wait for something to happen.

He moved to sit at his desk, and his hand fell on an oversize art book. *Rembrandt: The Complete Paintings.* He flipped through the pages, looking at the pictures. He used to do this all the time when he was little. As an art teacher, his mom brought home tons of books like these. He never really read the words, but he always liked looking at the pictures. Before, when he used to like art, he would sometimes even try to imitate the master-pieces he saw. Turning the pages of the tome before him was strangely calming. He let the details of Rembrandt's art wash over him. Brightly lit faces that glowed out of

deeply shadowed back-
grounds. Intricate
laces and fabrics
that looked so real
he was sure that if he
reached out, he would
feel their texture. Human
faces so lifelike they appeared
on the verge of movement. A boat
tossed on an impossibly precarious wave. A sketch of a
man with some kind of beast pacing in front of him.

Motion drew Vincent's attention from the book.
Tight Braids was herding the girls out of the bathroom.
Each of them was now dressed identically in a school
uniform—white polo and khaki shorts. Their hairstyles
were also nearly identical, smoothed back in either a
neat ponytail or two braids. Last in line, Georgia was
the only exception. Her hair was much too short and
instead was slicked to the side and clipped away from
her face with bobby pins. It was the first time she looked
normal. Vincent was surprised to realize he actually pre-
ferred the quirky, bed-head version of his cousin over
this one. Since she was rubbing her arm, he assumed
that Tight Braids's stun stick had played a part in Georgia's transformation.

Vincent tapped a finger on the glass door and caught

Georgia's eye. "Stay with Lili," he mouthed. She nodded, and soon the line of girls exited.

A teenage boy entered. Vincent recognized him as the same one who had stunned him. The boy used his stick to tap on the cells. "Your turn!" he shouted as he made his way down the line, then gave Vincent a mocking smile. Another *buzz-click* sounded, and cell doors opened. Vincent waited for Stick Boy to pass back by before opening his door.

"Try not to get tied up again," Stick Boy called, then broke into a cruel laugh.

Vincent turned and was surprised to see Ravi. Vincent hadn't expected him to actually be a captive in one of the cells. The boy glanced at Vincent with pursed lips, then looked away. Vincent followed him into the bathroom, planning to keep his distance.

Once the boys were ready—Vincent now in a matching uniform of his own—Stick Boy herded them to a cafeteria. Here, the boys and girls were again kept apart. Girls at one long table on the right, boys at another long table on the left. At least Vincent could keep an eye on Lili and Georgia.

Ravi motioned for Vincent to sit by him, but Vincent

chose a seat as far away as possible—he wanted nothing to do with that little sneak.

With their matching uniforms and hairstyles, the twentyish kids in the room looked like students at a small boarding school. Except, instead of teachers, there was an older group—teens and maybe a few in their early twenties—who were clearly guarding them. Four of them sat at a table at the head of the room. Two patrolled up and down between the girls' and boys' tables, stun sticks tapping menacingly in their hands. This was more like a prison.

Vincent noticed that not all the guards were dressed like Tight Braids and Stick Boy—in blue uniforms, with black sashes across their chests and stun sticks in their belts. A few of the older ones didn't wear uniforms at all. But while they looked like major threats, none of them really seemed old enough to be in charge. If the Distortionists had been around a long time, shouldn't there be some actual adults around too?

And what was their plan for all these kids? Where had all of them come from? It was a pretty diverse group. They all were speaking English, but Vincent picked out several accents among them. He didn't know much about the Distortionists beyond what Uncle Leo and Georgia had told him, but would they really keep their own kids in cells? Maybe these kids really had been kidnapped too. He wondered if any of them had tried to escape.

He looked over at the girls' table and tried to catch Georgia's attention, but she and Lili were deep in conversation with the girls around them. Georgia looked like she was thinking hard, and a spark of hope flared in his chest. She understood all this better than he did—maybe she'd work out a plan!

A sharp kick brought his attention back to his table. A freckled boy, a couple of years younger than Vincent, stared at him. "What's your name?"

"Vincent," he said and then cringed. He should have made up a name. He didn't want these people to know any more about him than necessary. He'd already been played by Ravi. He wasn't going to trust anyone here.

"Where did you come from?"

Vincent stared blankly at the boy. "Where did *you* come from?"

"Monet." The boy swirled his spoon through his oatmeal. "I almost drowned. Can't swim. I thought it was the best luck ever when the Lady saved me."

Monet? That was a painter, not a place. He must mean the painting he was found in. Like how Ravi had said "the Lady" found Lili in *Starry Night*. This was the second person to mention the Lady. And this boy thought whoever she was had saved him. "What's it like in here?"

The freckled boy shrugged. "I miss my mommy."

Another boy thwacked Freckles on the back of the head. "Shut up. You know what happens when you talk like that."

The other boy turned away, but Freckles seemed eager to talk.

"You gotta be careful not to break the rules here. Otherwise you might lose a meal or get locked in your cell all day." He lowered his voice. "I heard if you try to escape, they *beat* you."

Vincent gulped. They'd better not get caught, then. Getting shocked by the stun stick once was enough.

"So," Vincent asked, "are all the guards kids of Distortionists?"

"Distortionists? What's that?" Freckles seemed genuinely confused.

A bell dinged, and the children rose from their seats, returned their trays, and lined up in two separate rows by the door, girls on the right, boys on the left.

Vincent started to cross over to check on Lili, but someone caught his arm. It was Ravi.

"Girls and boys don't mix until sparring time."

Vincent shook off Ravi's grip. He had no intention

of listening to Ravi, but one of the guards walked by, buzzing a stun stick, and he didn't try to break out of line again.

Another bell dinged and the lines lurched forward.

Vincent just hoped that whenever they did mix with the girls, Georgia would have a plan to get them out of here.

He shuffled forward, feeling as trapped as the painted man from *Corridor in the Asylum*.

14

The boys were corralled into a white-walled room plastered with posters of famous paintings, several of which he recognized like *The Scream, Whistler's Mother,* and *The Persistence of Memory.*

Vincent couldn't imagine having to sit in this room day after day. He'd avoided art for the last two years, but this was the kind of art that would make *anyone* depressed.

Twelve desks in neat rows faced a smart board lit up with the words *Post-Impressionist Artists.* Great—this really was going to be like a boarding school.

Vincent slumped into a desk in the back of the room, and Ravi slipped into the one next to him with a timid smile.

Vincent was tempted to switch seats, but what was the point? He'd been captured by a secret society of magical art thieves, who were forcing him to go to school during spring break, and it seemed like the guy who'd gotten him caught wanted to be his new BFF.

The teacher was one of the older guards without a uniform. He had a wispy goatee and circular glasses. Stick Boy sat in the back of the room. Vincent guessed he was the assistant, probably keeping an eye out to make sure none of the boys fell out of line.

"Apparently we had a new student arrive last night in a rather unconventional manner," the teacher began in a stern British accent. Vincent glanced around. Everyone was staring at him. "Tell the class your name."

"Vincent." He'd already told Freckles. No point in hiding it now.

"Like Vincent van Gogh," the teacher continued. "Those are some big artistic shoes to fill. Typically new students are brought in by the Lady, but Ravi can help you find your way."

Ravi gave the teacher a thumbs-up. Great—now Vincent was officially paired with the person he wanted to be around the least.

"Let's start with something basic to get our new student up to speed," the teacher said, addressing the class. "Who can tell us, What is art?"

Vincent shrank in his seat as eager hands lifted all around him. *What is art?* Georgia had asked him a similar question when they were in the water mill painting. When he used to paint with his mom, he'd never thought about what art was. He'd just made it. Georgia had said art expressed truth and beauty. That it was a gift. But what did that really even mean? All he knew was that art had hurt him and let him down. He didn't know what art was anymore, if he ever had.

Vincent refocused on the class as the teacher turned to the whiteboard and wrote *Art = Power.*

"The first thing a country does when they conquer another is to either take or destroy its art. Because art is power. Every culture has known this. They tell their stories through art, their version of the world, of history. But we"—the teacher motioned to the class—"we know there's even a deeper power behind art."

A chill ran down Vincent's spine.

"Art is the power to move freely. To take what you want, to be infinitely wealthy. And, greatest of all, the power to influence the minds of the populace." The teacher turned his focus back on Vincent. "You are here because you—as does every child here—possess this ability. Our goal is to make you strong so you can take what you deserve."

The teacher continued his lecture, but Vincent was too busy replaying the way the teacher talked about art and power. It made him nauseated. He may not be interested in painting anymore, but using art to control people to get what you wanted was classic villain behavior. He eyed the other boys, wondering if they were just as uncomfortable, but they were all listening in rapt silence.

"You need to pay attention," Ravi whispered. "And try to follow the rules. You do that, and you earn points. Points earned equals privileges. More freedom."

"How many points do you need to kidnap a girl and rob a museum?" Vincent asked with a sneer.

"It's not like that," Ravi said, sounding hurt. "I'm trying to help you."

"Why?" Vincent scoffed. "Feel bad for ratting me out and getting us caught? I bet you got plenty of points for that." He couldn't believe Ravi was still playing innocent when they'd be safely back at Uncle Leo's if it weren't for him.

The teacher shot a warning look at them.

Ravi pursed his lips. When the teacher turned his back, Ravi said, "You're one of us now. Get used to it."

Vincent wouldn't accept that. He just needed to blend in until he saw a chance to grab Lili and Georgia and get out of here. Now if he could only get Ravi to leave him alone . . .

"Your sister shouldn't have been mixed up in that heist," Ravi said, still in a whisper but more defensively.

"The Lady dropped her with us on her way to meet the buyers—she's selling a big Rembrandt in a couple days. Jason was supposed to bring Lili back here, but he didn't want to miss the job. So I made sure she was okay."

Vincent opened his mouth to respond, but apparently the teacher had had enough of their chatter.

"Ravi, when I asked you to help Vincent, I didn't mean during class," he said, giving them another stern look. "Vincent, you may be new, but the Lady expects everyone here to learn the ropes and to learn them fast. Don't let her be disappointed when she returns and you have your official orientation." It was clearly a threat, but Vincent didn't care. He didn't plan on staying for orientation.

After the teacher droned on for a few hours about different conquests and how art had played a role in them, a bell sounded and class was dismissed. Stick Boy led them to a gym with a climbing wall, ropes course, and sparring mats. A couple of guards stood at the door, but the environment seemed more relaxed here than in the classroom.

The girls were already there, and Vincent spotted Lili,

who was holding hands with another girl. Georgia was nowhere to be seen. Vincent jogged over to his sister. She reached for his hand and squeezed it.

"When do we go home?" Lili asked. "This is my friend Tanisha. She's six like me. I told her you'd rescue her too."

"Shh!" Tanisha glanced toward the guards. "They'll hear."

Rescue her too? Vincent hadn't even figured out how to get *them* out of here. But there was no point upsetting Lili.

"Where's Georgia?" he asked.

Lili pointed up. Georgia was climbing from rafter to rafter. She reached the rope closest to them and shimmied down. Paint was streaked across her cheek in the same place the clay had been when Vincent first met her. Had that been only a couple of days ago?

Before he could speak, a bulky guard with a shaved head blew a whistle. "Warm-up laps. Go!"

Vincent made sure to stay close to Georgia as they fell in with the others, grateful for a chance to talk without looking too suspicious.

"What were you doing up in the rafters?" he asked.

"Checking for ways out, of course," she said, "and trying to get my bearings. There are no windows, though. I did look out the vent and could see the sky.

My guess is that we're somewhere in eastern Europe. Maybe Russia."

"You can tell where we are by the sky?"

"I can tell what *time* it is by the sky. That and comparing the approximate time difference between here and Texas narrowed my options. I stayed up all night so I wouldn't lose track."

Vincent was impressed by how spy-like Georgia sounded, but he wasn't going to admit it. He wished he felt as calm as she sounded. Maybe it was because, unlike him, she had a plan.

He looked around to make sure no one was paying them any special attention. "So how are we going to escape? Lili's already wanting us to rescue her new best friend, too, which might be a problem," he said, nodding toward Lili and Tanisha jogging ahead of them.

"I've been talking with the other girls, and I think Ravi was telling the truth," Georgia began, not registering Vincent's wince at the name. "Some lady really is fishing these kids—the Wanderers—out of paintings, though I still don't get how they are Traveling in the first place." She leaned closer and whispered, "Vincent, I think all these kids really were kidnapped."

"So? It's not our problem," he responded. "We need to get Lili and get out of here. Let your parents worry about the rest."

"Maybe." She bit her lip. "But if we could get that painting back too . . ."

"What painting?"

"I think it's the one they stole from the museum. They had us—"

A shrill whistle interrupted them. "Nine and under to the rock wall. Everyone else, it's time to spar," the guard yelled.

The younger kids ran toward the back of the gym, where a couple of guards began fitting them into harnesses. The other kids gathered around a large mat in the center of the gym.

"Do you at least have an idea of how to escape?" Vincent asked as he and Georgia jogged to the mat.

"Not yet."

There were only about eight other kids in their group. Tight Braids was in charge here, and she gave a cruel smile as she called Georgia and Vincent to the center.

"I think our new arrivals should show us what they are working with," she said. "Ravi, face off with the boy."

Vincent wondered if Tight Braids knew that he'd already beaten Ravi. Either way, this should be an easy win. He glanced over to see who Georgia was paired with and grimaced. She had squared off with Tight Braids. Georgia was tall for her age, but this girl stood a good six inches taller, which hardly seemed fair. Maybe they were trying to teach her a lesson as the new kid, but then why match Vincent with Ravi?

The older girl smirked at Georgia. "You have something on your face."

Georgia flushed as her hand flew to her cheek. Tight Braids lunged, but Georgia recovered her composure, dodged to the side, and threw one leg out to trip her opponent.

Vincent started to smile, but the ground spun from beneath him, and he found himself flat on the mat, ears ringing. Ravi was on top of him, a smug grin on his face. The surrounding kids cheered.

"Lesson one," Ravi said. "Strike when your opponent least expects it."

Vincent shoved him off. That wasn't fair. He hadn't been ready. "You mean 'cheat.' You lost last time we fought, remember?"

"Unless that's what you were meant to think." Ravi stood, knees bent in a loose, ready stance. Vincent charged at him, but Ravi was quick. And he probably wanted payback for being tied up. Vincent cast a glance at Georgia. She seemed to be holding her own against Tight Braids. Maybe they had a chance at outsmarting and outmaneuvering their opponents, and not just in this match.

This time, Vincent saw Ravi coming and threw out

his arms, but Ravi slid to the ground, knocking Vincent's legs out from under him. Another cheer rose from the crowd.

"Lesson two," Ravi said. "Never fight fair."

"These sound like bad-guy rules to me," Vincent said, shaken. Maybe they were more evenly matched than he'd thought. "I guess that makes me the good guy. And good guys always win."

Ravi feinted, then ducked under Vincent's punch and kicked him from behind. Vincent hit the mat with a thud. Laughter and whoops resounded from their audience. He lay on the mat, breathing hard. Ravi had knocked him down three times in a row, and Vincent hadn't even touched him once. He might as well have been playing a video game's most difficult computer-controlled player. And Vincent was pretty good at beating CPUs.

"Maybe if the so-called good guys actually tried to help, things would be different," Ravi said before walking away.

Thud! Georgia went down hard on the mat next to him.

So far, they were outnumbered and outmatched. And if the kids were this well trained, what were the adults in charge like? How were Uncle Leo—who couldn't even Travel—and Georgia's parents supposed to stop them or even slow them down? It wasn't a fair fight. Not by a long shot.

Georgia stood and offered him a hand up. Tight Braids was already calling the next group of kids to spar.

"What are we going to do?" Georgia asked as they watched from the sidelines.

Vincent just shook his head.

15

ym time ended, and after a quick lunch, Vincent and the boys were led away from the girls and into a new room. Vincent started to prepare himself for another boring lecture, but this room didn't have desks. It was filled with rows of easels. They held paintings in various stages of completion, but all were obvious copies of the one displayed at the front of the art room.

It wasn't in the bright, sweeping style of the artist's later works, but Vincent recognized it all the same. *The Potato Eaters.*

It was van Gogh's most famous early work.

A group of peasants—one man and four women—sat in a dark room. They were gathered around a small table, sharing a platter of potatoes. One woman poured tea to go with the meager meal. No vivid blues or brilliant yellows here. This painting was mostly gray and brown, creating a nearly monochromatic look similar to a black-and-white photo. The only bit of warmth came from the oil lamp that hung from a rafter above the table.

The other boys made beelines to their easels and unfinished paintings. Vincent took an unsteady breath as he located the only easel with a blank canvas. A variety of paints and brushes rested on the small table beside it. Being held prisoner was bad enough. But now it felt like they had looked deep in his soul and found the perfect way to torture him.

A young woman with auburn hair called for their attention. "Time to continue your reproductions," she said, the stern edge to her voice erasing the pleasantness of her round face. "You've been working on your pieces from a photograph all week, but now you have a chance to copy from the real thing. You have four hours to complete your reproduction. The girls had their chance this morning, and so the closest replica not only gets points but also earns dessert for their group—boys versus girls."

Stick Boy approached Vincent and prodded him with his stick. "Since you are just getting started, you can come up to get a better view. But the painting is unframed, so don't do anything stupid." He glared at Vincent as if daring him to try something.

As Vincent walked to the front of the room, his eye caught a simple gilt frame leaning against the wall. It looked like a perfect fit for *The Potato Eaters*. This must be the stolen painting Georgia wanted to recover.

Vincent wasn't interested in retrieving stolen paintings, but this could be their way out! A painting and its frame in one place.

The challenge would be sneaking off to this room all together. Who knew when they would let the boys and girls mingle again? And if the door was locked . . . He didn't know where they had taken their bags with her lock-picking tools, but Georgia was resourceful.

Stick Boy prodded him again. "You done looking?"

Back at his easel, Vincent felt frozen. He hadn't really looked at the details of the painting when he had been close to it. Even so, his fingers twitched with longing as he held them over the paintbrushes. He hadn't stood in front of an easel in a long time, but his body seemed to remember. He pulled his hand back.

A hand touched his shoulder, and Vincent spun, feeling exposed. The teacher looked him up and down with pity.

"There's no point in starting a new canvas when you won't finish. One of the new girls got a good start on this one." She removed the blank canvas from his easel and placed a half-finished reproduction in its place.

"Uh, thanks," Vincent said, but she was already making her way back to the front of the room. He didn't want to paint. It had been so long, and the idea of painting in front of these people made his palms sweat. Despite everything, his fingers itched to pick up a brush and paint the way he used to with his mom.

"Start with the dark colors. You can layer light colors on top, but it's harder to go the other way around." Freckles, the chatty boy from breakfast, was at the easel next to Vincent, stroking a brush across his canvas. "They usually let the new kids fumble around for a while before teaching them. They like to see what you already know."

"Should you be helping me, then?"

Freckles shrugged. "I'm always in trouble anyway."

Vincent watched the boy a bit longer. Then he fumbled with his supplies. He was familiar with the oil paints—his mom believed in giving kids real art materials, not finger paints and grocery-store watercolors.

He squirted colors onto his palette: burnt umber, Prussian blue, raw sienna, lead white. The earthy smells brought memories bubbling up to the surface of his mind. He pushed them down, studied the painting he had to work with, then selected a brush. His hand trembled as he mixed colors. He had once imagined he could be a great artist like his namesake, and now, as he tried to re-create one of van Gogh's paintings, that old longing resurfaced. But he already knew he'd never be good enough.

His parents had encouraged his love of art for as long as he could remember. They had mostly let him explore and experiment on his own, but his mother often taught him new techniques when they painted together. And then in fifth grade, Vincent had entered the school art show. He'd been so proud of his piece. He'd spent weeks painting a castle rising out of the ocean, monsters and unicorns and other fantastical creatures peeking through its windows and climbing its spires. He'd been particularly obsessed with the art of Pissarro, Manet, and Cézanne at the time, and Vincent tried to capture the loose style of impressionism in his own work.

The joy of making it flooded through him for a moment before being slammed back by the shame that had followed.

He hadn't won, hadn't even placed. But more than that, he could still hear the taunts of his classmates. *Looks like a freaky Noah's ark. My five-year-old sister could have painted that.* And that's when he knew: He wasn't good. And he'd never be great. But worst of all, he couldn't trust his mom. She had always said his art was amazing. *You have a gift, Vincent.* But it was a lie. All parents told their kids they were good at something when they weren't.

But it was fine, really. Now that he knew he wasn't good enough, he didn't have to waste his life trying. He could just quit pretending he could be an artist someday and accept that he'd just have some boring office job like his dad when he grew up.

A nudge brought Vincent back to the present. "You should really start," Freckles said. "You don't want to lose points."

Vincent touched the brush to the canvas. He half expected to hear the mocking voices. But they didn't come. He began to paint.

When he used to paint at home, Vincent had felt free, almost like he could fly. But now he was ultra-conscious of each movement, each paint selection, each brush-stroke. At first his body moved mechanically, almost as if he were watching someone else painting. But his muscles remembered what to do. He fell into a state of flow, mechanically copying the painting without really thinking about it, and the reproduction took shape. His mind wandered while he worked.

Why did the Distortionists train kids to paint? Did the Restorationists once train in the same way? Did Georgia's parents train her like this? Had his mom actually been training *him* when she taught him how to paint? Uncle Leo had seemed to think so. But no, that couldn't be right. She'd hidden this world from him on purpose. Why train someone for something you planned to never let them be a part of?

A new thought occurred to him. Had she actually held him back from being a great artist? Could he have fulfilled his dream if she'd let him be a part of this world?

He glanced at the kid next to him, whose painting was shaping up nicely despite his young age. "Hey, Freckles."

Freckles turned and rolled his eyes. "My name is Benjamin."

"What do they do with all these paintings?" Vincent asked.

Benjamin shrugged.

"How often do you copy paintings?"

"Almost every day. Till we graduate, at least."

"Graduate? Like till you're eighteen?"

Benjamin shook his head. "It's not an age. The Lady will tell you in your orientation, but once you get all the skills—or if you're a loyal thug—you graduate from being a Wanderer to a Spelunker. They get rooms without locks and get to go on missions and stuff. Unless you're special."

"Special?"

Benjamin pointed his brush at Ravi. "He's the youngest Spelunker, so he still takes classes. But the rumor is he's got some major *skill*."

He said the word with a special emphasis. Almost like Georgia did when she talked about Gifts. Was Benjamin talking about the same thing?

"What kind of skill?" Vincent pressed.

Benjamin shrugged. "Whatever it is, the Lady treats him like a prince."

Vincent's stomach growled. They'd been painting for hours.

"Time's up!" the instructor called. The boys moved to stand at the front of the room. Vincent put down his brush and joined them while the round-faced instructor walked through rows of reproductions, occasionally stopping to scrutinize one.

The Potato Eaters was within arm's reach. All he'd have to do was shuffle backward, touch the painting, and hope that he could Travel without the frame. Georgia said it was possible—it just would be harder. But there was no point in trying. He wouldn't leave Lili and Georgia. They just needed a way back to this room.

"Well, what a surprise." The teacher interrupted Vincent's thoughts. "It looks like we have a new prodigy. Congratulations, Vincent. Twenty points. The boys have earned dessert tonight."

Several boys whooped, and someone slapped him on the back. Vincent stood in mute unbelief. Not only had his painting been the best—and a lot of these kids were just as good at painting as sparring—but his peers were also cheering for him. For painting! His ears grew hot, but he couldn't help grinning. Only Ravi's sullen stare brought back the reality that these were the bad guys.

But surely there wasn't any harm in enjoying being the best for once.

Dessert was good. And having his accomplishment announced to the whole dining hall was only slightly embarrassing. Lili grinned and clapped wildly while the other girls groaned at their lost prize. Georgia just raised an eyebrow and looked thoughtful. Vincent wasn't going to bother worrying about what she was thinking. He was going to enjoy eating his brownie and ice cream and enjoy success for once.

Vincent scooped a big bite of brownie into his mouth. Ouch! The hot brownie scalded his tongue. He nearly spit it back out, but he managed to painfully swallow the giant bite of molten chocolate. He licked ice cream off his spoon, trying to cool his tingling tongue. No matter how sweet this small victory had tasted, it would burn him in the end, just like art had in the past. He ate slowly, lost in his own thoughts, as the other boys chatted.

After dinner, Tight Braids led the kids back to the "storage" hallway with the glass-walled cells, where they were allowed to linger before bed. After making sure Lili was okay—she was still glued to Tanisha's side—Vincent waved Georgia to a quiet corner.

"Any ideas?" Georgia asked.

"The painting we copied today," Vincent said, "the frame was just lying on the floor. If we can get back to that room . . ."

"Speaking of painting"—she nudged him—"you've

been holding out on me. There were some really excellent painters in our class that you beat out."

"Whatever." He didn't want to talk about painting with Georgia now or ever. "Do you still have your lock-picking—"

Georgia's eyes had gone wide. He felt a tug on his sleeve.

"Hey, your painting was awesome." How long had Benjamin been standing there? Had he heard what they were talking about? "Where did you learn to paint like that?"

The door banged open, and Stick Boy waltzed in, followed by Ravi, who now wore a black sash over his school uniform.

Tight Braids smirked. "Out of the doghouse?"

"He's on probation," Stick Boy said, shoving Ravi, "for incompetence."

Apparently the two teens thought this was hilarious. Ravi rolled his eyes, then scanned the room until he saw Vincent. Ravi walked toward him, and Benjamin scrambled away.

"The Lady wants to see you. Let's go."

Vincent swallowed. Why just him? Didn't Georgia and Lili also need to have their orientation? Neither of them had mentioned meeting the Lady yet, and he wasn't sure he wanted to meet the mysterious woman in charge of this creepy place—and maybe even the whole Distortionist organization—on his own.

Georgia looked significantly at Vincent as she pulled out a bobby pin, opened it with her teeth, and adjusted it in her hair. He hoped that was a signal that she could use her bobby pins to pick locks.

Vincent followed Ravi past the cafeteria, classroom, art room, and gym, past the hallway leading to the conference room where they'd entered this bizarre place, and into a hallway he'd never been in. To the left were several doorways, and Vincent thought he recognized some of the teachers' voices coming from them. Maybe those were their rooms. Ravi led him to the right, where only one door stood at the end. It was red with ornate carvings on it.

Ravi knocked and waited. There was a buzz, the lock clicked, and Ravi opened the door. He motioned for Vincent to enter the room but remained in the doorway.

Stepping into the large, L-shaped room was like stepping into a whole new world. The whole building had been drab and utilitarian, but this place was full of color and texture. Oriental rugs spread over dark wood floors, an ornate screen sectioned off a corner of the room, and groupings of plush furniture with intricately carved legs filled the space. And the paintings. The walls were covered in them—a few of them actually framed, including a large seascape. He wondered if Ravi realized that this was a mistake. He'd just shown Vincent the perfect way out, their escape route!

"Glorious, aren't they? I'm selling the Rembrandt in a few days, so enjoy it while you can." A woman in high heels clicked into the room from a door Vincent hadn't noticed. A woman who looked impossibly like—

"Mom?"

16

Vincent's mind reeled. His mom was the Lady everyone had been talking about with such awe? His mom was a Distortionist? Was this why she had hidden this world from him?

Mom smiled and walked toward him, heels clicking against the wood floor. But Mom never wore heels. And the black dress, the red lipstick, the smug smile. It was all wrong. Like an evil, looking-glass version of his mom. An avatar that had stolen her skin.

He took a step back.

"You're not my mom."

"Aren't you a clever one? I could use a smart boy like you around here." Fake Mom smirked. "Though I am surprised we are getting to finally meet."

She studied Vincent's face while his mind reeled.

"I have been fishing children out of paintings for

years, but imagine my surprise when I came across a little girl who called me 'Mommy.' I didn't think too much of it at the time, but to return from a meeting to find two other children have tumbled into my facility in an adorable rescue attempt!" She paused and scrutinized Vincent for a moment. "And yet I was certain my sister would never allow her children to get mixed up in all this Restorationist nonsense." It seemed she spoke these last words more to herself than to him.

Vincent stood, stunned. "Sister? No. Mom's sister died in a fire when I was a baby. So did my grandparents . . ." He trailed off. Because how else would this woman have his mom's face?

"Things aren't always what they seem." Fake Mom—or, rather, his *aunt*—walked to a cushy armchair by a window and gestured for Vincent to sit in the one across. "Come, nephew. Have some tea while I tell you a story."

Vincent followed, dazed. Mom never spoke about her sister. She didn't even keep photos of her. He hadn't realized they were twins. He didn't even know his aunt's name. He sank into the chair and, through the window, caught his first glimpse of the outside world since they'd been captured. It was late evening, and a city skyline glowed in the distance. Georgia probably would have recognized the city immediately. But Vincent had no idea what clues to look for without her help. He sank lower under the familiar feeling of uselessness.

His aunt pushed a small button on her chair, and a moment later, Ravi entered.

"Please bring tea for my guest," she told him. Her voice was smooth like a polished gemstone.

Ravi's eyes widened as he glanced at Vincent, but he only nodded before scurrying from the room.

Vincent looked at his aunt. His mom's twin. Not the end-of-game boss-level villain he'd been expecting. But somehow worse. He'd expected someone obviously evil, maybe even ugly or sadistic. How could he fight someone who looked just like his mom?

"I . . . I don't know your name."

A flash of pain crossed her face. "So my sister doesn't talk about me?" Vincent offered an apologetic shrug in response. "Call me Aunt Adelaide."

Adelaide. The name rang a bell. Vincent seemed to remember a French painter by that name with lots of perfectly posed portraits. It fit his aunt a lot better than his mom's name fit her. Artemisia Gentileschi was known for her fierce, sometimes-bloody paintings of courageous women. But his mom seemed afraid of everything, especially when it came to her kids.

Ravi returned with a tray filled with cookies, sliced cake, a steaming teapot, and two fancy porcelain cups.

He placed it on the small table between Vincent and Aunt Adelaide, who gave Ravi a nod of approval as he retreated. She poured a cup of tea, added cream and sugar, and handed it to Vincent.

He didn't even know if he liked tea, but he couldn't help glancing at the cookies.

"Go ahead and eat. I hear you've already had dessert, but an aunt is allowed to spoil her only nephew." Aunt Adelaide picked up a cookie, snapped a corner off, and popped it in her mouth. "I promise it isn't poisoned."

Vincent took a cookie and chewed slowly as his aunt poured herself a cup of tea and began her story.

"In grad school—you were just a baby—I fell madly in love with a brilliant young artist, Dorian. But, as it turns out, he was from the wrong sort of family—a Distortionist family, as my parents would say. They forbade our relationship." She twirled a strand of dark hair and stared out the window. "I thought we were Romeo and Juliet. He convinced me the fire was my only way out."

Vincent's body went cold. "You killed your parents to join the bad guys?"

"Join them? Ha!" Aunt Adelaide's laugh was full of bitterness. "Hardly. He used me to get what he wanted—my parents' directory of Restorationist families. The fire was to fake my own death. I thought my parents would get out. But Dorian had other plans. I stayed with the Distortionists for a while, but it was clear he had lost interest. I had to choose what was best for me. Play by my own rules."

Aunt Adelaide leaned back in her chair and stared at Vincent over her teacup. "I suppose, in her own way, my sister did the same by walking away from it all. When things got dangerous, she wanted to keep her children safe. Sheltered." She smirked. "But Traveling runs in our blood. We've been given magic in a world of weaklings. She's robbed you of that experience. But maybe it's to your advantage. You can see the world as it is, without all this good-and-evil dogmatism. You don't have to throw your life away on this never-ending fight. You can choose your own path. Don't let her rob you of that."

Vincent wondered again what it would have felt like to grow up knowing he had magic running through his blood. It did feel like his mom had stolen something from him by hiding this world. But the Distortionists really were evil—Aunt Adelaide's descriptions had only confirmed that. So her disdain of them made him curious. And none of this answered the question he and Georgia had been asking all along. "So if you aren't part of the Distortionists, why are you kidnapping kids?"

Aunt Adelaide tsk-tsked. "Dear Vincent, I've never done anything of the kind. The children in my facility were wandering around paintings and Corridors, completely lost. I rescued them. I have a talent for that, it seems."

That matched up with what Ravi and Benjamin had told him, but . . . "Lili didn't need rescuing," he said, then squirmed as he realized this wasn't exactly true.

Aunt Adelaide waved her hand dismissively. "By the time I suspected who she was, it was far too late to return her. I had an operation running through van Gogh and a meeting I was already late for. I wouldn't purposefully have taken any of my sister's children."

"So you're going to let us go?" Vincent gripped the edge of the chair, willing her to say yes.

Aunt Adelaide rose and retrieved a canvas from behind the decorative screen. "I feel a deep responsibility to all the children in my care. I only want to train them to their full potential. Speaking of which . . ." She propped it on her chair so he could see it.

Was that his copy of *The Potato Eaters*?

She tilted her head and appraised the reproduction. "It shows promise. I can see why you won. But it lacks emotion."

Vincent felt himself deflate at her final verdict. So it

wasn't that great. Just better than the others. At least she didn't try to hide the truth from him.

"I'll need to see more," she continued, "but it's possible you have a real talent. Not just an everyday skill like most in this world—a Navigator like my sister or a Restorer like Leo—but something powerful." She leaned forward. "I have a rare talent myself, which makes me the only one with the skills and knowledge to train you. You could be my apprentice, nephew. I could make you a real Artist."

A spark of hope chased away his earlier despair, and Vincent's skin tingled. A real artist? That old dream resurfaced like a tidal wave, powerful and terrifying.

But no! He shouldn't be listening to Aunt Adelaide. She may not be a Distortionist, but whatever she was wasn't *good*. That was obvious. He couldn't—shouldn't—trust her.

Vincent looked away from the painting to find his aunt studying him. Seeing that mirror version of his mom's face unnerved him.

Aunt Adelaide pressed the button to summon Ravi again.

"Please escort my nephew back to his room."

Ravi's eyes widened at the word *nephew,* and Adelaide held a finger to her lips, as if warning him to keep this information to himself. He glanced warily at Vincent.

It was clear he was being dismissed, so Vincent stood and began walking toward the exit.

"Oh, and one more thing, dear nephew. There's no need just yet for you to tell your little cousin about me— yes, I know who she is. It will be our secret while we discover your true talent. If she learns my identity, I'm afraid letting her go will be impossible. Earn my trust, like Ravi has, and you'll receive all the same privileges and more. Understand?"

Vincent nodded, unsure what else to do. He followed Ravi down the hallway in a daze. His aunt, alive. His aunt, a villain. His aunt, able to make him an artist.

Georgia was one of the few kids still awake, but Vincent avoided her gaze as he followed Ravi to his fishbowl cell and stepped inside. Too many conflicting thoughts and emotions tumbled through him, and he feared that if he looked at her, Georgia would be able to read them all through his eyes.

If they were really stuck here—for now at least— would it be so bad to let Aunt Adelaide train him as an artist? Being a Restorationist, trying to save the world, seemed like so much pressure. He didn't want to steal paintings, but maybe he could convince Aunt Adelaide they didn't need to. Maybe if he let her train him, he could convince her to let Lili and Georgia go. Maybe he could really have everything he wanted.

He tensed. Have everything he wanted? That was exactly what Aunt Adelaide had believed before the fire. What would that choice cost him?

He lay on his cot, but whenever he closed his eyes, all he saw were flames.

17

The next morning, Vincent's footsteps dragged. Adding the secret of his aunt to their already-uncertain fates brought an unexpected weight to the pit of his stomach. He hoped Georgia had an escape plan, because his brain was too distracted from his conversation with Aunt Adelaide to think of anything else. He'd talk to Georgia during the sparring lessons.

The boys were led to their first class, and Vincent realized his assumption that today would be the same as yesterday was wrong. Instead of the classroom, he found himself in the art room. The easels were stacked against the wall with several bags laid out in front of them. *The Potato Eaters* was gone, and a single framed landscape of a hilly green field stood on an easel at the front of the room.

A framed painting!

Vincent wiped his palms on his pants. This might

be a better way out than *The Potato Eaters* and less risky than breaking into his aunt's rooms.

"This is going to be epic!" Benjamin's voice pulled Vincent from his thoughts. The younger boy's face was full of glee. "We are going to wreck that painting."

"What?" Vincent asked, his voice rising in panic. Just when he had found a clear way out, they were going to wreck it?

"Attention!" The round-faced painting teacher walked into the room and positioned herself next to the easel. "Today you'll be working on booby traps, both creating and overcoming them. I will place you in two teams. You will each wear a harness, as it would be unfortunate to lose any of you during a training exercise." For the first time, Vincent noticed what looked like rappelling gear stacked against the opposite wall. "After your harness is secure, please take a supply bag."

Vincent ended up on a team with Benjamin and five younger boys, while the other team consisted of Ravi and a group that was clearly older. The groupings didn't seem fair, especially when Stick Boy decided to "join the fun" as part of Ravi's team.

Ravi's determined eyes met Vincent's. This seemed like a recipe for disaster.

When all the boys were ready, the teacher directed them to enter the painting. Once inside, she began a lecture about the technique of creating never-ending holes and instant oceans. Vincent stood in the back of the group, shifting uncomfortably in his harness. His aunt might not be training future Distortionists, but it didn't seem like the work they did was all that different. Vincent had no desire to encounter either of the things the teacher was describing, harness or no.

He was only a few steps from the entrance to the Corridor. Maybe he should make a run for it now. Could he make it to a museum, somehow get back to Uncle Leo's, then let Georgia's parents rescue the girls? At the very least, he should scope it out and have something to report to Georgia.

Vincent took a small step to the right. No one seemed to notice. He took another. The teacher droned on. She was demonstrating something with a paint tube, her attention focused away from Vincent. He took a final step.

The blackness of the Corridor enveloped him. His eyes began to adjust, but instead of glowing windows lining the hallway, this Corridor held dim images. Only the painting he'd just emerged from was brightly lit. Maybe his eyes hadn't fully adjusted, or perhaps the Luminescence was different Corridor to Corridor. Vincent stepped into the nearest painting and froze, shocked.

What once had been a beautiful flower-strewn field sloping down to a tree-lined river now stood desecrated.

Cusswords were painted along the dirt path, black holes dotted the grass, and a crudely painted raven sat on the lowest tree branch, grotesque and lifeless. A heaviness hung over the painting as if it were in mourning.

Vincent recalled the view from the Corridor. This definitely wasn't the artist's original work. These were clearly Distortions. Probably the aftermath of a lesson similar to the one he'd just escaped. The destruction of this painting gnawed at him. Someone had loved this scene enough to paint it. The memory of those kids mocking Vincent's art rushed into his head. This kind of destruction was different, but it felt the same.

"There's no way out, you know." Vincent spun to find Ravi staring out over the field. "She's not dumb. These don't lead anywhere." Ravi pointed to the empty wall behind them, where a window to the outside world should have been. There was none. It struck Vincent now why all the paintings in this Corridor were dim: None of them were framed.

"Who's the artist?" Vincent wasn't sure why he asked.

Ravi shrugged. "No one you would have heard of. Hid their art away in an attic. Never showed it to anyone. Not everyone with the skill of an artist is famous."

Ravi picked up a stone and tossed it into one of the black holes. Vincent listened for the sound of it hitting the bottom, but none came.

"But this is wrong. Art is meant to be . . . appreciated, not destroyed." Just because someone didn't want to share their art with the world didn't mean they wanted their art scribbled all over. It was like defacing a gravestone.

"You think I don't know that?" There was an anger in Ravi's voice that surprised Vincent. He held up his hands to indicate he meant no harm as Ravi approached him.

Ravi was scrawnier than Vincent, but Vincent now knew that the kid was faster, stronger, and specially trained by a criminal mastermind. There was no one to stop Ravi from throwing Vincent into one of these holes and never looking back.

"You act like you're the good guys, but I don't see

your kind fishing kids out of paintings," Ravi said. "I do what it takes to survive. And so should you."

Vincent realized what really bugged him about Ravi was that he claimed to have been kidnapped but it seemed like he bought into Aunt Adelaide's whole framework. At least kids like Benjamin wanted to go home. "Don't you miss your family? Have you even tried to escape?"

Ravi looked away. After a while, he said, "I was four. I'd been wandering the streets in London. I don't remember how long or what happened to my parents. Snuck into the Tate to get warm one day, and when I saw the art, I felt like I was home. Don't know how I didn't get kicked out looking like I did." A ghost of a smile crept

onto Ravi's face. "There was this one painting that was calling me. When I touched it, I thought I'd died and gone to heaven. And then she was there. Like an angel. That's what I thought at the time."

"What do you think now?"

Ravi stared at his hands. "I think I do what I have to."

Vincent wasn't sure why Ravi had opened up to him, but he couldn't let Ravi's sob story or Benjamin's or any of the others get in the way of his mission. All he wanted was to get Lili and Georgia and go home.

He pushed past Ravi into the Corridor and stepped back into the first painting, not bothering to be discreet. The instructor gave him a half-amused look, then continued lecturing.

"It's unlikely any of you will be able to successfully paint your way out of a hole or other booby trap," she was saying. "A true Artist can paint whatever they envision and have it come to life. They can even supersede the forced perspective created by the original artist and touch any part of the painting, however distant it seems."

Forced perspective. That was the way artists created the illusion of distance in their work. A canvas is a flat, two-dimensional object, but with forced perspective, an artist could make mountains, buildings, or anything else seem far off in the distance.

But standing in a painting was different. Things

weren't flat at all—the perspective wasn't forced. Those mountains really were miles away. At least, Vincent thought so. It seemed impossible for anyone to touch them without hiking for hours. The instructor said a true Artist could. But Vincent was no artist, even if his aunt thought he had potential, so trying seemed pointless. Still, the instructor had caught his attention.

"Even without the skill of an Artist, painting your way out of a situation is worth trying. You just need other strategies. For instance, you can scrape paint off and toss it at your opponent's face." She held up a palette knife and scraped it against a Distortion she must have created earlier in the lecture. "If you do fall into a trap— let's say a never-ending hole—you could possibly even scrape out ledges to use as footholds or handholds so you can climb back out. Although I'd suggest you don't rely on that technique to save you. Scraping isn't easy when you're falling, and I have yet to see any student successfully achieve it." The smug look on her round face reminded Vincent that this wasn't an average art lesson.

"However," the instructor continued, "*you* should be the one leaving the booby traps for your enemies."

Several boys chuckled and whispered to one another.

"Experience is the best teacher, so let's have our new student, Vincent, face off against Ravi." Ravi's team slapped him on the back, and the teacher directed Ravi's and Vincent's teammates to grab hold of the ropes attached to their harnesses. Vincent felt numb. Someone placed a palette knife in his hand. Ravi cracked his knuckles and pulled a paint tube from his pocket.

"Wait—what am I supposed to do?" Vincent asked the teacher, panic mounting. This exercise suddenly seemed very dangerous.

"Think of it like a game of tag. You're it, and Ravi will use any means possible to evade you. Tackle him—your team gets a point. Fall down a hole—lose a point." She blew a whistle. "Go!"

Vincent noticed a hole to the right of the teacher—he must have missed that part of the lesson—and sidestepped away from it. Vincent shifted his weight, but Ravi didn't move. He took a deep breath and ran straight toward Ravi. Maybe this would be easy like their first fight. Ravi didn't try to dodge. He merely grinned, pointed the tube in his hand at the ground in front of him, and squeezed.

A large black spot appeared in front of Vincent and spread toward him like slick oil. A new black hole. If Vincent had realized they were so easy to create, he wouldn't have run at top speed. He tried to simultaneously dodge and leap over it and ended up tumbling forward. He braced himself, half expecting to splat into the wet paint, but instead, he plunged into darkness. His stomach flipped at the roller-coaster-like drop before the painful jerk of his harness stopped his fall. Vincent sighed in relief, thankful that his team had a good hold on the ropes. He hoped they wouldn't let go.

Falling down a never-ending hole would be a horrible way to die.

His teammates helped him out of the hole, and the instructor had him and Ravi face off again and again. Each of Vincent's attempts to tackle Ravi or avoid the new holes was equally unsuccessful. He tried using his palette knife to scrape out ledges, but he could manage it only while dangling and waiting for his team to haul him back up. The instructor had been right about it being impossible while falling. He wished he hadn't skipped the earlier part of the lesson. Maybe then he'd know how to stop Ravi and avoid falling in these holes.

It was five to zero, with Ravi's team ahead, when the instructor had them switch and it was Vincent's turn to set traps. He filled his pockets with tubes of inky black paint from a supply bag. As far as he could tell from watching Ravi, the tubes were designed to burst when squeezed firmly.

The instructor blew her whistle, and the boys squared off again. But even though the painting was already ruined, Vincent hesitated to squeeze his tube of ink, not wanting to harm it further. Twice Ravi tackled him, winning more points for his team. When Vincent finally did squeeze his tube, it backfired, coating his hands and shirt in black and leaving only a small hole in front of him. Ravi tackled him again. Another point.

Finally, another two boys were called to face off. While none of them did as miserably as Vincent, his team continued to trail Ravi's in points. The training game continued several hours with a short break to eat pre-made sandwiches from their packs. The boys left their trash scattered around the painting or tossed it down never-ending holes.

Eventually the instructor blew the final whistle. "Ravi's team are the winners and will receive dessert tonight. You have thirty minutes to play before you must return your supplies and line up for dinner."

Vincent sat on a large rock to catch his breath while the other boys took off in different directions within the once-beautiful painting. The training had taken place in the center, about a hundred meters in, so none of the never-ending holes were close to the Corridor or where anyone would enter the painting from the real world. Vincent felt sick as he watched the other boys create Distortions.

Some painted lifeless bugs and birds. But most were

more interested in graffiti, eager to leave their marks on this little world.

Mom had told him that all people wanted to leave their marks and that some people thought that was the whole point of making art. But she believed the best art was created when artists forgot about themselves and just focused on the truth they were trying to capture.

He closed his eyes and remembered painting like that, thinking only about what he was creating. Would he ever be able to paint like that again? He opened his eyes and studied his ink-stained hands. Another reminder that he'd always be a failure.

18

The moment Vincent entered the gym after dinner for free time, Georgia led him to the empty climbing wall.

"Best option for privacy," she said, climbing quickly.

Vincent scrambled for handholds to catch up. "Tell me you have a plan to get out of here."

"Was *The Potato Eaters* still in the art room?"

"I didn't see it, but it could have been in the closet."

"Still, that doesn't help us get there without being seen." Georgia stopped and looked down at him. "But listen—nothing adds up. I talked to a lot of the other kids after you were taken away last night, and all of them claim to have gotten lost in paintings, the same way Lili did. And Lili said she went with a lady she thought was your mom. She seemed confused about it, but, Vincent, what if that's why your mom didn't want you to know about the Restorationists?"

"No way." Vincent scrambled up the wall till Georgia was eye level. "My mom is not involved in kidnapping or stealing paintings or whatever else this group is doing." Although the truth—that his aunt was kidnapping kids and training them for some unknown purpose—wasn't much better.

"Look, I don't think these people are Distortionists— the training is weird, and there are no real adults—so what if she started a third group? Maybe it's her way of getting revenge for her parents' and sister's deaths?" Vincent didn't like the wild "I've got it all figured out" look in her eyes.

"My mom's not like that."

"But she basically lied to you about the family and about Traveling! And why else would she have quit doing missions—"

"Stop! You don't know what you're talking about." Vincent's stomach clenched as tight as his fingers on the handholds. Even if Georgia didn't have all the information, accusing his mom was crossing a line.

He took a deep breath. "Lili's a little kid. It was dark in the painting and the Corridor. She was probably just scared and confused. My mom may have stopped being a Restorationist, and she may have kept this world from me, but she would *never* be involved with stealing and destroying art. She just wouldn't."

As confused and angry as he felt, this was one truth Vincent was sure of. His mom *loved* art. That was the whole reason she'd sent him and Lili to Uncle Leo's. She'd taught him everything he knew about art and painting. She hadn't just taught him—she'd made it part of their life. Painting on rainy Saturdays. Looking through art books together. Sketching pictures at the park. She'd made him love art, too, at least for a while. It wasn't fair for Georgia to accuse his mom. She didn't know Mom. She didn't know any of them.

Georgia shrugged and continued to climb while Vincent rested his forehead against the cool wall. He could tell Georgia about his aunt. He could clear his mom's name right now. But Aunt Adelaide's parting warning rang in his mind. It was probably better he kept his aunt and her offer to himself. Besides, as soon as they got out of here, Aunt Adelaide wouldn't matter anymore. But he could give Georgia enough information to make her stop accusing his mom.

"I met the lady in charge last night."

Georgia paused her climb and descended until they were eye level. "And?"

"Well, she does kind of look like my mom. I can see how Lili would be confused."

Georgia looked deflated. "What else did you learn?"

Vincent racked his brain for something he could tell her without revealing too much. "She said they aren't Distortionists. That she just finds missing children and brings them here."

"And you didn't think to mention this earlier?" Georgia sounded annoyed.

"You didn't give me a chance the way you went straight to accusing my mom! And now you want to blame me?"

"I'm sorry. I—"

"I'm going to check on Lili." Vincent descended a few feet, then dropped to the ground. Georgia called after him, but he ignored her.

Vincent found Lili playing with Tanisha.

"Hey, Lili. Let's talk," he said, waving her over. She stood, Tanisha's hand gripped in hers. "Alone, I mean."

There was a short protest, but in the end, Lili joined him as they walked a few feet away and sat down.

Vincent looked her in the eye. "You shouldn't get attached. We're getting out of here as soon as we can."

"I know," Lili said, "but Tanisha's coming with us. She thinks she lived in California, too, and she misses her mommy and her cat."

He sighed and poked Lili's tummy. "I'm just in charge of getting *you* home safe."

She swatted his hand. "Don't. I'm a big kid. I can help. I learned lots of things today. Like don't touch the frame of a painting when you're in the big dark place."

"I learned that one the hard way." He gave her a small smile, but a knot of worry formed in his stomach. Escaping would be hard enough without his sister demanding he rescue her new best friend.

"Let me redo your hair, Lili," Georgia said, plopping down beside them. "I miss my clay, and my hands need something three-dimensional to work with. Painting isn't the same."

"Don't you like painting?" Lili asked as she scooted into Georgia's lap.

"I like looking at paintings and Traveling into paintings," Georgia replied. "And my parents made sure I know my way around an easel, but sculpting and pottery are what I really love."

"My teacher tells us to follow our dreams. Do you want to do pottery instead of growing up to be a Restor—what did you call it?" Lili asked.

"Restorationist." Georgia looked thoughtful. "I can't imagine a world where I stopped sculpting. There's a part of me that's meant to create things. But following that dream couldn't ever be more important to me than protecting people and art. Being a Restorationist is . . . a calling."

Was this why Georgia doubted his mom? Did she feel Mom had walked out on that calling? Would Georgia accuse him of the same thing if he decided not to be involved with the Restorationists when they got out of here? His aunt had certainly walked away when she chose to create whatever this place was. He thought back to her offer to train him to become a real artist. Ever since stumbling into *Starry Night,* he couldn't shake the feeling that art was a missing piece of him and that he'd been walking around with a hole in his chest for the last year and a half. The last few days had opened that wound again and again.

But Georgia didn't get it. She had something she was good at. In fact, she had lots of things. She didn't know how painful it was to realize you couldn't do the one thing you'd set your heart on.

"If you don't focus on pottery, won't you feel like you gave up on something you were meant to do?" Vincent asked. "Most artists dedicate their whole lives to becoming the best."

Georgia didn't immediately respond but continued to braid Lili's hair. Finally, Georgia said, "Do you know the story of the artist Lili is named after—Lilias Trotter?"

"I do! I do!" Lili almost popped up in excitement, but Georgia's fingers in her hair steadied her.

Georgia laughed. "Then tell us."

"This famous painter guy said Lilias could be the greatest painter ever if he taught her, but she went to Africa instead to help people there."

Mom loved to tell them about the artists they were each named after. But there was something about Lilias's story that bothered Vincent.

"Giving up her art to help people makes her a good person and all, but didn't she miss out?" he asked.

"That's the thing." Georgia finished the braid that now circled Lili's head like a crown, then began undoing it to restore her approved ponytail. "She didn't actually give up her art. She felt that God had called her to help people in Africa, but she also continued to paint— really beautiful paintings—while she was there. Stuff she never would have painted if she'd stayed in England. The only thing she really gave up was pursuing fame."

She turned to Vincent. "There's a difference between making art and making a name for yourself. Making art focuses outside yourself, on the art itself and the people who will experience it. Making a name for yourself just focuses inward, on what the art can do for you."

Vincent hadn't thought of art in that way before.

His art teacher in elementary school had told them art was self-expression. His mom had just encouraged him to create, but he'd never really thought about *why* he painted. He'd definitely never been focused on who would experience his art—at least, except for wanting people to think he was talented and praise him. And when the opposite had happened, he'd just stopped.

A new thought struck him. "Is that what makes a painting able to be Traveled through? Because the art has something to say to the person looking at it—like the artist is inviting us in, not just showing off?" He certainly hadn't been trying to communicate anything in his copy of *The Potato Eaters*. Maybe that was why Aunt Adelaide had said it lacked emotion and wasn't as good as it could have been.

Georgia nudged his shoulder. "Look at who's suddenly interested in art! Now we just need to figure out your Gift."

Vincent tensed. Aunt Adelaide had said he could be an artist, but had she actually been referring to what Georgia called Gifts—an Artist who didn't just create art but who had some special abilities? Either possibility felt too private to share.

Lili bounced in Georgia's lap. "I want a Gift! What's mine?"

Vincent was relieved by Lili's interruption.

Georgia chuckled. "It can be hard to tell until you're a little older, but you could be a Navigator, a Restorer, an Appraiser, a Tracker, or even an Artist."

Lili leaned her head against Georgia's chest. "I want to be what you are."

Georgia wrapped an arm around her. "You're going to be whatever you're supposed to be."

Vincent felt a pang of jealousy, both for Lili's affection and for the way she connected with people so easily.

"Ravi!" Lili cried. "Come hang out with us."

Much to Vincent's chagrin, Ravi approached slowly.

"Ravi told the best jokes after the Lady left me," Lili said. "I thought she was Mommy at first, but she never came back, so now I don't think so. I was really scared, but he made me feel better. And I told him about you, Vincent, and I said you would be good friends. You, too, Georgia."

Why did his sister have to like everyone! Couldn't she tell this guy was bad news? "Lili"—Vincent glanced up at Ravi—"you can't just be friends with everybody."

"He's not *everybody*! He helped me!" She rolled her eyes, then widened them in excitement. "We should bring him with us, too, when we go home."

Now it was Vincent's turn to roll his eyes. Lili was too little to get it. Ravi had done nothing but cause more problems for them. And if they didn't escape soon, she was going to keep trying to add to their rescue party.

"Do you want to play dodgeball?" Ravi suddenly asked Vincent. "We need one more to make it even."

"Not my problem," Vincent responded.

Ravi looked surprisingly hurt as he walked away.

"That was cold," Georgia said.

"Yeah, that was not nice," Lili chimed in.

"We need to focus on getting out of here," Vincent said. "Nothing else matters."

He thought he meant it, even as he tried to quiet the echo of Adelaide's words in his head. *I could make you a real Artist.*

19

At the end of the day, Vincent found himself escorted by Ravi to Aunt Adelaide's room while the other kids were herded back to their cells.

He sat on a plush sofa, staring at another tray with tea and cookies while he waited for her. Did she expect to win him over with more stories and treats? Her attention gave him an unsettled feeling.

He finally took a cookie covered in powdered sugar and was just biting into it when Adelaide came briskly into the room, heels clicking.

"So, nephew"—she walked up to the sofa and took a seat uncomfortably close to Vincent—"tell me about your art."

"My art?" The cookie stuck in his throat, and he drank some tea to choke it down. "We don't really have . . . I mean, we just have prints. No art like . . ." He trailed off. He'd been about to say "Uncle Leo." Was this a trap? Would that be giving things away? Or would she already know what art he had?

Aunt Adelaide laughed. It was the kind of laugh you might use when trying to reassure a little kid. "No, darling. Tell me about *your* art."

Vincent felt his face flush as he realized what she meant. It seemed that he couldn't escape being asked to talk about his art. "There's nothing to tell. I used to paint, but I wasn't that good. So I stopped." Making art with Mom had been his favorite thing. And she'd praised his every attempt to emulate the great artists she taught him about. But she'd also said his piece for the art fair was perfect. He couldn't trust what she thought.

Aunt Adelaide smiled. She leaned closer. "Here's what I think. You may be an Artist. Not just someone who can paint, but an Artist powerful enough to create paintings that others can Travel through. Someone powerful enough to alter the realities within a painting."

Of all the Gifts Georgia had explained to him, Artist seemed least likely. Aunt Adelaide must not have heard how badly he'd done in training today. He'd failed miserably at altering anything within that painting. "I'm not an Artist."

Aunt Adelaide stood and motioned for Vincent to follow her. "Prove it." She led him around the ornate folding screen to a corner of the L-shaped room that was set up like an art studio. An easel stood waiting with a prepared canvas, and a small table next to it held an assortment of paints and brushes. The palette was already loaded with dollops of paint.

Adelaide draped an apron over Vincent's neck. He felt cold, and his hands were slick with sweat. He couldn't do this. He'd just make a fool of himself to one more person. He'd never be good enough. *And what if she says you are good enough?* A small part of him said that was what he really wanted.

The apron strings cinched around his waist as Aunt Adelaide tied them from behind.

He clenched and unclenched his jaw, wiping his sweaty palms on the apron. "What am I supposed to paint?"

"So serious, nephew." Her voice was silky. "Relax. Paint what makes you happy." She placed her hands on his shoulders. "Or perhaps what makes you angry. Any emotion will work."

He closed his eyes and blew out a slow breath. Memories washed over him. Mom's hands on his shoulders as she called him "my artist." Drawing silly pictures to make Lili laugh. But then came the ugly taunts of his classmates. His cheeks flushed with shame again. He'd hidden his art away, given up. But then, at Uncle Leo's house through the wonder of *Starry Night*, art had started to call to him again. But he was still so afraid of not being good enough. And now they were trapped, maybe forever.

And whose fault was that? His aunt's for creating this nightmare school? Ravi's for turning them in? Georgia's for leaving the door unlocked? His mom's for hiding this world?

The fear was gone, and in its place, Vincent found only anger. He was angry at this whole out-of-control situation. Anger had been boiling under the surface, but he couldn't keep it from churning up anymore. He loaded his brush with dark gray and slapped it onto the canvas.

He was angry that he couldn't keep Lili safe. Angry that Ravi kept picking on him and that his aunt wanted something from him. Angry that Georgia had ever left the room unlocked for him and Lili to wander into *Starry Night* in the first place. Angry that he couldn't just be happy painting anymore, that it all had been ruined that day at the art fair. Angry that his parents had kept this whole magical, amazing, terrifying world a secret instead of handing him his birthright. That's what this was—his birthright. His skin tingled as he lifted the brush again and again.

Finally, he stepped back and stood, breathing heavily. Had he been painting for minutes? Hours?

"Your anger is intoxicating, nephew," Aunt Adelaide whispered in his ear. "I'm going to train you to be the most powerful Artist in a generation." She kissed him lightly on the cheek, then clicked out of the room.

Vincent stared at what he'd created. The face of a furious dragon stared back, and it looked ready to devour him.

It had the pull. It wasn't as strong, but it was the same pull he'd felt with *Starry Night* and other paintings they'd Traveled through. Vincent backed away from his creation.

Images of laughing with Mom while painting flooded his mind. Some of those paintings had had a kind of pull as well. Even if they weren't technically the very best. Even if not everyone liked them. Had he always had this power? Had Mom known and hidden that truth from him?

He'd pushed down his longing to be an artist for so long, but it had never really gone away. And now it resurfaced more powerfully than ever. If Aunt Adelaide was right, she could help him become a real Artist. That missing piece was within reach.

He stared at the dragon, feeling the heat of his own anger reflected in every brushstroke. It was powerful, but it was also terrifying. This wasn't who he wanted to be.

Aunt Adelaide wouldn't just train him to be an Artist. He would be her canvas, and she would make him a reflection of herself: angry, spiteful, and cold. He would become something he hated, and so would his art.

Vincent dropped his palette and brush on the floor, then yanked off the apron.

As Ravi led him back through the building, Vincent's insides were screaming. He had to get out. They had to get out of here. Now. No matter what.

When Ravi opened the door to Vincent's cell, Vincent paused as his hand touched something unexpected in his pocket.

"I just wanted to thank you for teaching me rule number two." Vincent's fingers wrapped around a tube of ink from today's training.

Ravi scrunched his brows. "What was that?"

"Never fight fair." Vincent whipped the tube out and squeezed it in Ravi's face. Ravi threw his hands up, but it was too late. Black ink flew into his eyes, and Vincent shoved him into the cell, then quickly shut the door.

Vincent ran to open Georgia's cell. She jumped up from her cot, wide eyed.

"Quick," he whispered. "Hold Lili's door open while I grab her. Can you pick the lock to the art room?"

"Yeah." Georgia yanked the bobby pins from her hair.

Lili was fast asleep on her cot. Careful not to wake her, Vincent picked her up, grateful she was a sound sleeper and small for her age. He headed for the door.

"What about the other kids?" Georgia asked.

Benjamin was awake. He banged on his cell door and looked pleadingly at Vincent. Other kids started to stir.

"No time," Vincent said, pulling his gaze away. "We have to go now."

Georgia bit her lip but followed as Vincent hurried out of the room and down the hallway. Should they try for one of the paintings in his aunt's room? No. Getting caught there was too great a risk. And the conference room was too close to his aunt's. Of all the exits, their best option was *The Potato Eaters*. He hoped it was still in the art room.

Vincent glanced up and down the hall while Georgia unbent a bobby pin with her teeth and fiddled with it in the lock. He adjusted his grip on Lili, willing her to stay quietly asleep.

"Got it!" Georgia swung the door open.

"Hey!" Stick Boy stood at the end of the hallway, in pajamas and without his stun stick. He glanced behind him. He seemed uncertain whether he should chase them or get help.

"Go!" Vincent said, shoving through the door, which Georgia locked behind them.

The painting that the boys had wrecked that morning still sat on an easel at the front of the room.

The doorknob rattled, and pounding reverberated from the door. Vincent couldn't fight while holding Lili—not that he was a match for Stick Boy, even without the stun stick. He didn't have any more clever tricks up his sleeve either.

"It's here!" Georgia pulled *The Potato Eaters* from the closet and laid it carefully on a table. She looked at it longingly. "Too bad we can't take it with us."

"Just hurry," Vincent said as the banging on the door continued. Stick Boy's voice called out for help.

She ducked back into the closet and emerged with a frame. "Hopefully this is the right one." When she lowered it onto the painting, it fit snugly.

The banging grew louder, as if someone were kicking the door, then stopped completely. They needed to get out before Stick Boy came back with help.

Keeping one hand tightly around Lili, Vincent reached for the painting. Thankfully, he landed on his feet in the dark, crowded room. The painting's inhabitants let out surprised exclamations, but neither Vincent nor Georgia took any notice as they bolted into the Corridor.

Georgia led the way down the dim passage, until Vincent remembered something that stopped him in his tracks. "Wait—what about the Luminescence?" he asked, adjusting Lili in his arms. "They'll be able to see exactly where we went."

"Then we have to go somewhere unexpected," Georgia replied.

20

"Do a couple of quick hops to leave a false trail while I find the right gateway." Georgia's shadowy form hurried down the Corridor, pausing briefly at various paintings.

Vincent's heart pounded. His arms were starting to ache. He wasn't sure how many paintings he could jump through while holding his sister, even if landing on his feet was getting easier. But Lili was always grumpy when she got woken from a deep sleep, and by the time he could explain what was going on and get her moving . . . Well, they didn't have time for that.

Vincent reached out his hand and stepped into the first painting. Just a slight stumble, but not enough to wake Lili. He ran back into the Corridor and into another painting.

"Georgia?" he whispered after exiting a third.

"I hope you've got lots of energy, because we have a ways to go." Her voice came from behind him. "Come on."

She led him into another painting a little farther down the Corridor.

Georgia immediately swung around and studied the window to the outside world. "I'm not sure what time it is, but I think the museum must be closed. It's dark, at least."

"Which museum?" Vincent asked.

"Van Gogh in Amsterdam," she said. "It's the easiest to get to, and I know what hop we can make next. The room is clear."

"This seems like a bad idea. There could still be cops."

"Which makes it an even worse idea for them to follow us."

They stepped into the museum. They were on the smaller top floor this time. Voices echoed up through the central balcony, but no one seemed to be nearby.

"Georgia," Vincent whispered, "I don't think the museum is closed."

"Of course it's closed." She peeked over the parapet and drew back. "It's just that it's still a crime scene."

Boots landed with a clomp behind them. Vincent turned to see Stick Boy with a smirk on his face. The round-faced painting teacher appeared beside him. They both held stun sticks.

"Run!" Georgia raced down the stairs, Vincent at her heels.

His running jostled Lili, who started crying, but Vincent didn't have time to worry about soothing her.

They flew past the level full of police and yellow tape.

More boots sounded behind them, this time with accompanying shouts. They kept running, but Vincent risked a glance back as they rounded a corner of the stairwell.

One cop was hot on their trail, but Stick Boy and the teacher had been halted in their pursuit and were wrestling with two other officers.

"Hard left!" Georgia shouted as they reached the ground floor.

Vincent tightened his hold on Lili as he dove into the painting his cousin led them to. When they collapsed on a dirt path, he loosened his grip on his sister and struggled to catch his breath.

"Why does it feel like things keep getting worse and worse?" Vincent's whole body was shaking from adrenaline. Lili was still sobbing, and Vincent tried to shush her as gently as the tremors in his arms would allow.

"Worse?" Georgia said. "If those cops hadn't been there—"

"That was too close." If the cops hadn't been there, Stick Boy would be dragging them back to Aunt Adelaide right now. "Do you think that cop saw us jump?" He stood and peered through the window to the museum. The cop was already hurrying to the next room.

"Even if he did, he'd think he was crazy. No way he would tell anyone."

"What if they send more people to find us? Don't we need to keep moving so they can't track us by the Luminescence?"

"That's the beauty of this painting." She gestured for him to take a look.

They were at the bottom of what looked like a dry riverbed, with high banks on either side. Everything except the robin's-egg-blue sky was painted in shades of mud brown, even the trees. A cow lowed as it ambled down the path toward them. The familiar strokes and colors of van Gogh were nowhere to be seen.

"It isn't a van Gogh," he said, realization dawning. "Aren't all the paintings from the museum his?"

"Nope. This is *The Sunken Path* by Jules Dupré. Which means it connects to a different Corridor. Which means they have no way to track us. And we're almost home."

Lili finally stopped crying and looked around. "Where are we? What happened?"

"Everything is going to be okay," Vincent said. "We escaped, and we're almost home. Or back to Uncle Leo's, at least."

Lili looked around. "Where's everyone else?"

"What do you mean?" Georgia asked.

"The other Wanderers? Tanisha and Ravi and everyone." Lili looked back and forth between Georgia and Vincent, panic filling her features. "Why would you leave them?"

"It's complicated," Vincent said. "We didn't have a lot of time, and we didn't really know who we could trust. Those kids were probably brainwashed."

"No, they all wanted to get out too. They miss their families." Lili's eyes shone with tears. "How did you get out?"

"I . . ." His ears grew hot. What he'd done to Ravi suddenly seemed cruel rather than clever. "I tricked Ravi and trapped him in my cell."

Fresh tears streamed down her face. "Poor Ravi's going to be in so much trouble."

"Lili, these people are very bad," Georgia said. "And Ravi was working for them."

"I know! That's why we have to go back and rescue everyone! Ravi too." She crossed her arms, face set in a determined expression.

Georgia rubbed her temples and began to pace. Vincent lay back down on the ground, exhausted and exasperated.

"This sounds like a problem for the grown-ups to

solve," he said. "Let's get back to Uncle Leo's, and we can call the police."

"Except I never figured out for sure what country we were in," Georgia said. "And the police can't exactly follow directions through paintings."

"Then your parents can deal with it," he shot back.

"Can they do that?" Lili asked. He didn't like how she looked at Georgia like she was the hero even though he was the one who had gotten them out.

Georgia rubbed the bridge of her nose. "It's unlikely anyone is going to get back in the same way we got in *or* got out. They'll almost certainly unframe all those gateways. I'm sorry, Lili, but I didn't see any other framed paintings." Lili sobbed harder, and Georgia gathered her into a hug. "Don't worry. I'm sure my parents can figure it out."

Georgia may not have seen any other framed paintings, but Vincent had. He tried to picture the ones in Aunt Adelaide's sitting room. He had seen one of them somewhere before. If he described it to Georgia, she'd probably recognize it. But there was no way he was telling the girls. He wasn't going back there for a bunch of kids he didn't even know. Especially if it endangered his family. He wasn't a hero. And they weren't safe yet.

Vincent watched as Lili cuddled up in Georgia's lap,

turning away from him. He had done the right thing, hadn't he? Lili would understand. Eventually.

They stayed in the painting long enough for Georgia to feel confident that they'd have a smooth journey home. She was taking them through the Met.

"Is going through another museum a good idea?" Vincent asked as she led them through the Corridor. "We don't need to be chased around by guards yelling in English this time."

"That's why I had us wait. The museum is closed. This is going to be a piece of cake."

The only part of the Met Vincent had previously seen was the storage room, and he tried to take in as much as he could while Georgia led him and Lili through the space and into an exhibit featuring the art of Norman Rockwell.

"My parents were supposed to take me to this exhibit," Georgia said quietly, a bit of sadness tingeing her voice. "Rockwell is one of Gramps's favorite artists."

Vincent had never really paid attention to Norman Rockwell's art before. As they walked through the exhibit, he was fascinated by Rockwell's people, who looked both hyper-realistic and humorously exaggerated at the same time.

They snuck through a painting of a snoring postal worker and into the Corridor.

"Now we just have to find Gramps's painting, and we're home!" she said.

They walked several minutes until they reached a painting displaying a man carefully fitting a stained-glass window together. An artist at his work. It wasn't humorous like many of the other Rockwell paintings. The man's posture on the scaffolding and the angels in the glass window conveyed a level of reverence.

"Here we are. Our gateway home," Georgia said. "A lot of the art in Gramps's house belongs to museums or private collectors, but this one, he owns. He actually met him once."

Vincent gaped at her. "Uncle Leo *met* Norman Rockwell?"

"Who's Normal Rockwall again?" Lili asked.

"Norman Rockwell," Georgia corrected. "And he's one of the most famous American artists. This painting has been in the family since Gramps was a young man."

How cool was that? Uncle Leo getting to meet one of America's greatest artists.

They stood staring at the painting another minute. Then, without a word, they stepped into it.

They found Uncle Leo pacing in his studio. He was a disheveled mess, and judging by the Texas-sized coffee mug—which looked like it might have been one of Georgia's early creations—he hadn't slept since they left. And he wasn't happy to learn they had rescued Lili alone without tracking down Georgia's parents. He went on a long rant about the risk to their lives and how their parents would never trust him again, setting Lili off into more tears, and then he stomped outside to get some air. After the kids found something to eat, Vincent carried a sleepy Lili to bed.

When he came back downstairs, Uncle Leo had barricaded himself in his studio, and Georgia was sitting at her wheel, elbows braced on knees, mashing the spinning clay between wet fingers. Vincent plopped into a chair beside her.

"I can't decide if I just want to go home and be safe and forget all of this ever happened . . ."

"Or?" Georgia stretched the spinning clay into an impossibly high tower.

"Or if I want to do this every day," Vincent said. Just a few days ago, he'd wanted nothing to do with art. But now he found himself wishing, despite the trials of the last two days, that Traveling through paintings with his family could be a part of his life. He couldn't be an Artist—that terrifying dragon had shown him that. But maybe he could be a Restorer like Uncle Leo. Or find something else he was good at. He wouldn't be ready to say goodbye to this world when his parents picked him up. "I mean, it must be exciting to go on missions with your parents. Doing something important and magical. You're so lucky."

She smashed the clay down into a lump again and shut off her wheel. "Yeah. Lucky me." Her sarcasm surprised him.

"What? You don't like it?"

"The thing about missions . . ." She trailed off as if she'd meant to say more, then changed her mind. "Yeah, you're right. It's pretty awesome to get to make a difference," she continued flatly. She plopped the lump of clay into a five-gallon bucket and began wiping the wheel with a rag. "What are your parents going to think about all this?"

"I have no idea. I mean, I know they're kind of obsessed with keeping us safe, so I don't think they're going to be too happy. I just feel like they could have trusted us with the truth instead of lying to us all this time."

Georgia wrung the rag without looking up. "People hide the truth for a lot of different reasons."

Vincent glanced at his cousin. Did she know he was hiding something? He didn't even know why he was still keeping Aunt Adelaide a secret. But just the thought of her reminded him of his own potential to become something he hated, the shadow version of himself lurking beneath the surface. And that was something he wanted to keep hidden.

The secret seemed like a sudden wall between him and Georgia. A wall he'd built himself.

21

At breakfast, Uncle Leo was back to his normally gruff self, but Vincent could tell he was no longer angry at them.

"It was a foolhardy thing to do." Uncle Leo speared a piece of French toast and transferred it to his plate. "But it was brave and selfless. And to be honest, those are the qualities a good Restorationist needs in spades."

Vincent didn't feel brave or selfless. He'd tricked Ravi and run off without even trying to rescue the other kids. He guessed that was the opposite of what a good Restorationist was supposed to do. Uncle Leo was wrong about him.

That afternoon, while Georgia gave a giggling Lili lessons on the wheel, Vincent borrowed supplies from Uncle Leo and sketched for the first time in a long while. First he drew the wildflower-strewn field visible from the enclosed porch. Then he sketched the girls at the wheel with Lili's wobbly lump of clay.

He wasn't sure if he trusted himself to paint these scenes when he got home, but a sketch was a good way to remember. His thoughts roamed back to Aunt Adelaide's school and the kids still there. Before he realized what he was doing, he'd sketched Benjamin, Tanisha, and even the scowling face of—

"Is that Ravi?" Lili seemed to appear out of nowhere at his shoulder.

She tilted her head. "He shouldn't look angry. He's scared."

Scared? Ravi walked around that school like he owned the place. Benjamin had said Ravi got special privileges, and it was clear to Vincent that the boy was Aunt Adelaide's youngest, most trusted minion. He could still see Ravi's smirk after he repeatedly tackled Vincent when they faced off during training.

Georgia leaned over, wiping her hands on a damp rag. "She's right. Ravi was kidnapped like all those other kids."

"He still had a choice," Vincent said. "He chose to turn us in."

"It's not that easy to switch sides." Georgia scratched her cheek, leaving a streak of clay in its characteristic spot. "He probably didn't think we could pull off a rescue by ourselves. It was less risky for him to report us."

Vincent started to voice his disagreement but instead cringed as he remembered his own safer choice to rescue only Lili and Georgia when he could have opened the other cells. It didn't excuse Ravi's choices, but it made them somewhat understandable.

"We're going to the river," Georgia said like she knew he needed a distraction. "Want to come?"

Vincent shook his head. "Just watch Lili, okay?"

"You mean you actually trust me?" Georgia said with feigned shock.

"I'm not a baby!" Lili crossed her arms.

Vincent smirked. "As long as there aren't any paintings to fall into at the river."

"Oh, I didn't tell you about the art display down there?" Georgia grinned.

"There's art at the river?" Lili asked, looking from Georgia to Vincent in confusion.

"Just God's art," Georgia said. "Race you!"

The girls took off out the back door in a tumble of giggles.

Vincent wandered the house, taking in the art he'd tried to ignore when he first arrived. Outside Uncle Leo's studio, he was drawn to a glass-topped curio table displaying miniature paintings. Across from it stood a wall of untidy bookshelves. Many of the shelves sagged with the weight of large art books.

He ran his fingertips along the books before stopping with a jolt of recognition. He pulled out the volume and stared at it. This was the same book from his fishbowl cell.

He plopped it on the floor and scanned its pages. Rembrandt was Dutch, like van Gogh, but his paintings were more realistic. He had a way of playing with light that created a contrast between a darker background and people who almost seemed to glow.

Vincent flipped pages quickly until he saw what he was looking for, then froze, heart racing.

He'd found their way back in. And it was impossibly dangerous.

"I keep thinking about the kids we left behind." Vincent turned from watching Lili, who was fast asleep, her arm hanging over Mr. Rumples, to look at Georgia. "We—I mean, I—should have helped them."

"I feel bad too. Hopefully my parents can figure it out, but we don't have much for them to go on."

Vincent looked at his hands. "I think I know a way back in."

"You saw another painting? A framed one?"

Vincent nodded. He stood and retrieved the book from his room, then flipped it open to the page he'd found earlier.

Georgia whistled. "This is from the Gardner Museum heist! It was the biggest art heist ever."

"When do your parents get back?" he asked.

Georgia shrugged. "A few days maybe?"

A few days couldn't hurt, right? Those kids had been there for way longer. And at least now there was a plan to rescue them. Days. A thought struck Vincent. Both Ravi and Aunt Adelaide had mentioned she was selling a Rembrandt.

"A few days might be too late," he said.

"Why?" Georgia asked. "It's not like the whole school is going to move."

"But this painting is." He explained what Ravi had said about selling the painting, deciding not to complicate things by mentioning Aunt Adelaide.

"Foiled again." Georgia flopped onto her back. "Wait." She sat back up. "When did you say this sale was happening?"

Vincent thought back, trying to calculate days. "I'm not positive, but I think tomorrow."

Georgia's eyes sparkled. "Are you up for another mission?"

Vincent's body tensed. He'd only meant to suggest this painting as a way for Georgia's parents to rescue the other kids. Uncle Leo's words rang in his head: *Brave and selfless . . . those are the qualities a good Restorationist needs in spades.* His dragon flashed before his eyes. Fear and anger. He couldn't become that person. He'd made a mistake in not freeing the other kids. But with Georgia's help, he could fix it.

He grinned. "We need a boat."

Their plan was simple enough. They'd Travel through Rembrandt to the framed painting at the school. Once there, they'd scout around for the stolen van Gogh. If they didn't find it quickly, they'd rescue the kids without it. They talked about looking for a safer painting to Travel home through, but Vincent had suggested they use the two pocket-size miniatures from the curio as their backup gateway to Uncle Leo's. They'd leave one on Vincent's bed and take the other with them. As soon as all the kids were through the miniature, they'd have to remove the frame so they couldn't be followed. The only downside to that plan was they'd have to leave the second miniature behind. Vincent was sure the little painting of a man in a lace collar couldn't be too valuable, but even if it was, hopefully Uncle Leo would think these kids were more important.

"Why is this even in here?" Vincent asked as he and Georgia set the canoe down just inside the third bedroom. They had found it in the upstairs junk closet along with an old satchel and art kit to replace the ones left behind when they escaped.

"Gramps never gets rid of anything," Georgia said. "Do we have everything we need?"

"We've got the canoe and oars. And I've got the satchel." It weighed down Vincent's shoulder, reminding him that he was stuck between wanting to be an artist and resisting it.

"I've got the note for Uncle Leo," a still-sleepy Lili said with a yawn. She kept Mr. Rumples snugly tucked under one arm as she rubbed her eyes.

"Don't fall asleep before you wake him up," Vincent reminded her.

"I won't." Lili looked at him sternly. "I'm not a little kid."

"I've got one miniature, and the other is on your bed." Georgia continued her checklist. "And I've got the trash bag to protect the stolen painting in case we find it."

Vincent bent down to hug his sister. "I want you to count to two hundred, then run and wake up Uncle Leo."

Lili nodded.

Vincent stepped into the crowded room with Georgia, swung the door shut, and turned the lock. He didn't want to risk Lili following them instead of giving Uncle Leo the note. On the other side of the door, Lili's unsteady voice began counting.

"Did you find a better route?" Vincent still wasn't sure how Adelaide had found Lili in *Starry Night*, but he didn't think it was safe for them to Travel through van Gogh. Luckily Georgia agreed and had searched through the stacks of paintings while Vincent wrote the note to Uncle Leo.

"Yup. It's seven o'clock here, which means . . . one o'clock in London, where we'll transfer to Rembrandt, and hopefully it's still three or four in the morning where we're headed." Georgia flung back the sheet covering a stack of paintings.

Vincent cringed.

The painting facing him was full of naked people.

22

"**N**o way am I going in there," Vincent said.

"Let me get this straight," Georgia said, arching an eyebrow. "You have no problem risking your life to go rescue the other kids, but you are afraid of walking through a painting with naked people."

"I'm not afraid. It's just . . ." Vincent rubbed his neck and looked away. He'd seen photos of nude paintings in books before, but they'd always made him uncomfortable, and he'd flipped past them quickly. "It's gross. I mean, why would someone pose for something like that?"

Georgia flushed. "I guess I hadn't thought of them like real people. Naked people are part of art. You get used to it. But maybe that's not a good thing."

She glanced at the painting again. "Still, this is the best route. I looked through as many paintings as I could, but time is ticking. We have to get to the school before morning, or we may as well not go."

Outside the door, Lili yelled, "Two hundred!" Her footsteps pattered down the hallway.

Georgia hefted her end of the canoe. "How about we hold this over our heads?"

Vincent laughed with relief. "Good plan."

The painting full of naked people was surprisingly easy to navigate. Vincent just kept his eyes on the ground and shuffled forward behind Georgia. Bare feet darted away from their path, and the gasps and exclamations of the painted people echoed strangely inside the upturned canoe. He sighed as they reached the blissful blackness of the Corridor.

"Where are we going, again?" Vincent asked. They lifted the canoe off their shoulders and flipped it over to carry it between them.

"The National Gallery in London," Georgia said. "There are plenty of Rembrandts once we get in. Here we are."

In minutes, they were inside the deserted National Gallery.

"Now, to find a Rembrandt," Georgia whispered. She

set down her end of the canoe gently, and Vincent did the same.

He glanced around the dimly lit room, and his eyes stopped on a particular painting. A dark room crowded with people in fancy clothing, perhaps at a feast. The painting centered on a robed king wearing a bizarre turban-crown combination, which didn't seem historically accurate for any time period. Every face in the painting was contorted in terror as a disembodied hand wrote on the wall in shining letters. Their panic pulsed in the air around Vincent, and the mysterious hand seemed to shimmer as the painting's dark background pervaded his peripheral vision.

"Hey, don't go without me."

Georgia's voice shocked him from his trance. His hand had been inches from the painting.

"I can't carry the canoe by myself," she said.

"Why does this keep happening?" he asked.

Georgia tilted her head. "It looked like you were under a spell or something. Maybe it's because you just started Traveling? Or it might have something to do with your Gift."

"I could almost see them moving." Vincent noticed the plaque next to the painting. *"Belshazzar's Feast.* It's a Rembrandt. Maybe that's my Gift."

"What? Accidentally locating paintings?" Georgia smirked.

Vincent shrugged. "It seems pretty useful. So what made Rembrandt imagine something like that? It looks like a horror story."

"It's from the Bible," Georgia said. She explained that the Babylonians had taken the Jewish people captive and looted their temple. Then they'd taken the Jewish holy items out during a feast. But a hand appeared and wrote a message on the wall, saying that God had judged them, and they were conquered by the Persians that very night.

The story reminded Vincent of what Uncle Leo and the wispy-goatee teacher had each said about different people groups stealing one another's art. But the floating-hand thing was pretty cool.

"I wish we had that kind of help," Vincent said.

"We *are* that kind of help. We're trying to be, at least."

Vincent stared at the painting. The people looked pretty panicked. "Is it safe to go in there? Maybe we should look for a different Rembrandt."

Footsteps sounded down the hallway along with the characteristic blip of a two-way radio.

"It's safe enough if we hurry through," Georgia hissed, grabbing her end of the canoe.

Vincent hefted his end. "That wizard hand is enough to make me hurry."

"Angel hand," Georgia corrected. "Come on." They reached forward together and stepped into chaos.

Women screamed. Food spilled from silver trays as servants shoved past Vincent. A young man cowered under the table, crying. Vincent watched the eerie hand trace shining letters on the wall. Over the scents of roasted meats and wine wafted the sharp smell of seared stone.

A vase flew by, inches from Vincent's face.

A bearded man pointed toward them, yelling. He hoisted a goblet and threw it at them. His aim was bad, and the goblet ricocheted off the canoe and hit the floor with a clang.

"This way!" Georgia pulled to the right.

A platter whizzed by Vincent's head just as he reached the Corridor.

They collapsed on the ground. Vincent's heart pounded, and he gasped for breath, even though they'd had to run only a few yards. They could have been seriously injured. Vincent ran his hands along the side of the canoe. It was dented in a few places with at least one small hole. Would it hold long enough for them to execute their plan?

He had a sudden disturbing thought. "When you said that if you die in a painting, you die, how certain are you about that? Are you sure you don't just get dumped back in the Corridor or something?"

Georgia shook her head. "This isn't some video game. Dying is a real risk."

"Are you really okay with risking your life for these kids?" he asked. What if they didn't want to be saved? Regardless of what Lili thought, he wasn't certain that Ravi did. Maybe all the kids had bought into Aunt Adelaide's vision of art and power.

Georgia stared silently at the canoe for a moment. "Risking your life to help people and save art is kind of what being a Restorationist is all about," she finally said.

"So you're not even scared?"

"Of course I'm scared." She looked away. "But fear shouldn't get to decide what I do."

Vincent looked back at the glowing image of *Belshazzar's Feast*. Those panicked people did exactly what fear told them—running, hiding, lashing out at those around them. He'd done what fear told him—squirting the ink at Ravi and shutting him in the cell. Then he pictured Lili. Her tears when she realized they'd left the others behind. She would have gone back right then, if she could, for people she barely knew. She would have been brave and risked herself to help them. He could do that for her. Fear couldn't tell him what to do.

"Which way to the sea?"

23

he Storm on the Sea of Galilee loomed before them. The glowing window revealed an overly crowded boat cresting a violent wave.

A group of men huddled in fear at the back of the boat. One man strained at the rudder while a handful of men worked to save their ship, but their desperate attempts to manage their torn sail and repair broken rigging looked futile.

When Vincent had examined the photograph of the painting in the art book, he'd thought the one spot of blue sky shone with hope. Skimming through this painting in a canoe had felt doable. But now the dark clouds seemed poised to swallow up any brightness. These men were doomed to failure, bringing down Vincent and Georgia's mission along with them.

No wonder Aunt Adelaide didn't bother unframing it. This was a suicide mission.

Vincent focused on a man wearing a blue cloak and a pink hat in the middle of the boat. Though one hand kept a tight grip on the rigging, he seemed calmer than the others.

"I feel like that guy's looking right at us."

"He is," Georgia said as she dragged the canoe parallel to the window. "That's Rembrandt."

"What? The artist? I didn't know he lived in Bible times."

"He didn't. But a lot of painters like to add cameo appearances into their paintings."

Georgia stepped into the canoe, tucked her oar under her chin, and gripped the boat's edge with one hand.

"What are you doing?"

"Trying to find the best position," she said. "I don't want to fall overboard when we splash down. We have to hold on to the canoe, or it might not come with us."

Vincent swallowed hard. He faced Georgia and tried to imitate her position, wishing their boat were more stable.

"Remember, we just have to not get swept away from the window."

"I know," Vincent said. "And if we see people in the

room through the window, we call it off and row hard to get back to the Corridor. Got it."

"Ready?"

He took a deep breath and nodded.

"One, two, three." With one hand holding tight to the canoe, they each reached out their free hand and entered the painting.

They hit the water hard. The impact bounced Vincent from a squat into a sitting position, jarring his spine. As he attempted to help Georgia stabilize the canoe, it tipped, sloshing frigid water over their feet.

Great. His shoes were wet again. But he didn't have much time to worry about that with the wind tearing at his clothes and hair. It screamed around them, drowning out all other noises. He squinted toward Georgia, and his stomach dropped as a massive swell hit their canoe, lifting them several feet into the air.

The wave passed, pushing them deeper into the painting and closer to the men in the boat.

Vincent looked over his shoulder for a glimpse into Aunt Adelaide's. The good news was that the room seemed empty. The bad news was that they would probably die trying to get to it.

They rowed fiercely, attempting to turn their canoe around. Georgia grimaced, clearly struggling. Another wave hit their canoe, and this time, it swept Vincent's oar out of his hands.

What was he supposed to do now?

It was almost ironic that he'd been running away from art so long when becoming an artist was the one thing he really wanted. And now art was going to kill him. How could he have been stupid enough to think that they could pull off this rescue? He just wasn't good enough. He was sure someone out there had some kind of art-rescue magic, but it obviously wasn't him.

With only Georgia to row, they drifted closer and closer to Rembrandt's boat, screams now adding to the violent howling of wind. A group of men were shaking one of their own, who was lying within the boat's hull.

Oh my goodness, the storm already killed one of them. We're all going to die.

"Vincent!" Georgia's yell snapped his attention back to their canoe, which was now rapidly filling with water.

"We're leaking!" Vincent yelled back.

"I know! Try and *do* something about it!"

Vincent cupped his hands and bailed out as much water as he could. The water swirling into the canoe was formed from individual brushstrokes and carefully mixed colors, but the wet chill on Vincent's hands told him this water could drown him just as easily as the actual ocean. And it was filling their canoe quicker than he could empty it. The water was above his ankles and rising.

More yelling came from the ship, distracting Vincent from his task. The motionless man hadn't been dead after all! The storm raged as fiercely as ever, but the man sat calmly even as the others continued to yell and cry out in fear. How could he look so peaceful when everything was falling apart?

Movement to the man's left caught Vincent's attention. It was Rembrandt—the painted version of him, anyway—waving his hat at Vincent. He was yelling something to him, but the little Vincent could make out over the screeching storm was definitely not English.

He wanted to yell a thing or two back at Rembrandt for painting this impossible storm!

Painting! Could Georgia fix the leak the way she'd fixed the waterwheel? The storm may have taken his oar, but perhaps she could paint him a new one or create a bucket to bail with. Or even better, maybe she could fix the canoe!

Vincent braced his legs against the boat and pulled the kit from his satchel.

"What are you doing?" Georgia yelled as another massive wave swelled under the boat.

"You can paint the hole closed!"

"What? You know I can't paint detail work. And *I* need to keep rowing! You do it!"

Another wave sent them into the air and crashing back down. He didn't have time to worry about whether he had the skill or was good enough—it was try it or die. Vincent spilled the contents into his lap. Brush clenched between his teeth, he squirted a tube of paint. He hoped color wasn't important. He just needed to shade in the hole and hope it worked. The water lapped at his shins as the boat continued to pitch, but he found the leak and got to work. Stroke after stroke, he painted. Water stopped seeping through as he created a green patch where there was once a gaping hole.

Vincent laughed out loud in disbelief. It worked! It really worked.

"Thank you!" he yelled, waving his brush at Rembrandt, who nodded back in approval. Another wave hit the canoe, nearly knocking Vincent overboard.

Right. This wasn't over.

It would probably be easier for Georgia to row if the canoe wasn't half-full of water. Could he make the water in the canoe disappear by painting over it? He'd finished the green, so he squirted out more colors and loaded his brush again. It took all his concentration to paint over the water as the waves kept rocking the canoe, but the water level began to drop. Soon it had even stopped sloshing. In fact, the boat had stopped moving altogether.

Wait. He couldn't have done that.

Vincent looked up to find that the surface of the water was as flat as a tabletop. The sun shone, and the howling wind had been replaced by a gentle breeze.

He turned to find Georgia gawking at the other boat, her paddle now still across her lap.

"What happened?" Vincent wiped his brush on his jeans and set it on the satchel.

She grinned. "We just witnessed a miracle—maybe two!"

"What are you talking about?"

"The storm stopping. That's the miracle this painting is based on. Jesus tells the wind and waves to stop, and they listen. But a painting is just a moment in time, imagined by the artist. Jesus calmed *this* storm. A real miracle."

The men had fallen silent and were all gathered around the former sleeper—Jesus. A real miracle. Until this moment, Vincent would have said he didn't believe in miracles.

His breath caught as Jesus looked straight at him. It was like Jesus could see into the depths of Vincent's soul: his anger at his parents, his decision to hide the truth from Georgia, the way he hadn't allowed himself to care about the other kids. That ugly dragon was who he really was on the inside. He felt more exposed than the people in that nude painting. He expected Jesus would turn away in disgust. But Jesus held his gaze, eyes soft and filled with love.

Warmth began in Vincent's chest and spread to his fingertips. He had the sensation that he was a canvas and Jesus was covering up all the wrong inside him with fresh paint. A new vision of who he could be emerged: a Vincent who was willing to help others even if it cost him, who was brave enough to make art, no matter what other people thought. Tears welled in his eyes. That was who he wanted to be. Jesus nodded as if in approval of their mission, and a swell of water pushed their boat right beneath the window of Aunt Adelaide's room. It hung within easy reach.

Vincent took one last look at Jesus. *Thank You,* he said silently, sure that he was heard.

"Whoa," Georgia breathed. "I've never seen anything like that."

"Yeah, I thought Rembrandt was nuts, but I get why he would put himself in this painting." Vincent paused. "Wait. You said 'two miracles.' What was the other one?"

"Finding your Gift at the exact time we needed it." Georgia grinned broadly. "You're an Artist!"

Vincent's heart skipped a beat. "What? I mean, I didn't do anything different from when you fixed the waterwheel." Hearing it from Georgia felt different from when Aunt Adelaide had said he was one, but he still wasn't sure he could believe.

"I watched you," Georgia said, shaking her head. "I've never seen the paint respond to anyone like that. It's like it *wanted* to do what you *needed* it to do. It was awesome!"

Vincent looked away, his ears growing hot. It had felt pretty awesome, the way the paint had done exactly what he needed. And unlike when he'd painted the dragon, he hadn't been filled with anger and self-pity, just determination to save himself and Georgia so they could complete their rescue.

"Ready to go?" Georgia asked, interrupting his thoughts.

"Sure." He looked down at the battered boat repaired with his multicolored patches. "I hope Uncle Leo wasn't too attached to this canoe."

Georgia patted the pocket of her overalls where the tip of the plastic bag holding the miniature stuck out. "Good thing we brought our own exit."

24

incent and Georgia crouched behind a plush sofa in his aunt's fancy room. He was painfully aware that his dragon painting might still be on the other side of the decorative screen.

"I think we're clear," Georgia said.

They started toward the door, but Vincent's damp shoes squeaked with each step.

Perfect. He slipped them off and headed toward the partition instead.

"What are you doing?" Georgia whispered.

"They squeak. We can come back for them later." He caught a glimpse of his dragon painting, still sitting on the easel, as he bent to tuck his shoes behind the screen.

"Anything important back there?"

"Uh . . . no." He couldn't let Georgia see what he'd

created, what was still inside him. Maybe Jesus could forgive him, but she'd never trust him if she knew.

He hurried to join her at the red door, but his stomach twisted, knowing his aunt held a painting connected to his darkest emotions.

They snuck down the dimly lit hallway, stopping occasionally to listen for signs of movement. It seemed they had timed things right, as all was quiet.

They soon reached the art room. Vincent hoped after the chaos their escape had caused that *The Potato Eaters* might still be there.

The room and all the easels were empty. But in the closet they found stacks of the students' attempts at recreating *The Potato Eaters*.

Georgia slowly flipped through them.

"You think the original is hidden with these?" Vincent asked.

"It has to be," she said. "They can't have sold it already. And why make all these copies if they planned to get rid of the original? I bet they'll try to pawn the copies as the real deal. Once, the *Mona Lisa* was stolen, and a forger sold six fake copies of it! If a painting is known to be stolen, buyers ask fewer questions. Let's keep looking."

"But it's not what we came for." Every second they spent here increased their risk of getting caught. "You can come back with your parents and look again."

"With my parents." Georgia laughed grimly. "What a joke."

Vincent stared at his cousin. "I don't get it."

She traced the edge of a canvas. "I thought, if I recovered the painting, I could prove myself. Show them I was ready."

"What are you talking about? Ready for what?"

"It's funny," Georgia replied, her voice flat. "Our parents aren't really that different. They just want to keep me safe. Too many Restorationists have died in the past decade." She turned to face him and sighed. "The truth is I've never been on a mission."

Vincent gaped. "And you're telling me this now?" He'd put so much of his trust in this girl, who seemed to know everything, who could do everything.

"I should have told you—I almost told you. It was just so nice to have someone really believe in me for once." She turned away from him, her shoulders shaking.

Was this what she meant when she was talking about secrets yesterday? Vincent couldn't stay mad at her. Not with all the secrets he still held back. It made him want to confess everything about Aunt Adelaide. About his fears—and maybe his longing—about being an Artist. Georgia had been in the same boat as he was all along, and he never even knew it. They didn't have much time, but he needed to help her past this.

"You pick locks. You know the locations of thousands of paintings in dozens of museums. You repaired a painting while spinning on a waterwheel. You teach my sister pottery. You volunteer for a suicide mission without hesitation just because it's the right thing. You're brave, and you care about people. I've never seen anyone do the things you can do. Even if your parents can't see that yet, they will. Even if they don't believe in you yet, I do. You have more potential than everyone I've ever met combined." Vincent stood, waiting for a response.

Georgia sniffed, swiped at her nose, and turned around. "So you don't think I'm just your weird homeschooled cousin?"

"Are you kidding me?" he said with a grin. "You've been homeschooled this whole time?"

She half smiled. "You are pretty dumb."

He rolled his eyes. "So should we try the conference room?"

"No," she said. "Forget the painting. Let's save those kids."

They stepped into the dimly lit hall of glass-doored rooms. Ravi lay asleep in the first cell, drooling slightly.

He had a busted lip, and the skin around his eyes was bruised and swollen. "What happened to him?" Vincent whispered to himself. Had Ravi been punished for their escape?

Vincent still didn't trust Ravi, but if they didn't help him, who would? Vincent pictured his sketch from earlier that day—he had seen Ravi one way, but Lili still saw good in him. Vincent's mind flashed to his last look at Jesus in *The Storm on the Sea of Galilee*. Jesus had seen the worst parts of Vincent and still offered acceptance. Georgia was already opening the first cell on the girls' side of the room. Vincent made his choice. No matter what Ravi had done, he didn't deserve to be trapped here.

The door creaked as Vincent pulled it, and Ravi's eyes popped open. They were so bloodshot that Vincent recoiled. The paint. Ravi's face wasn't bruised—it was stained from Vincent squirting paint at him.

Ravi scooted back on his bed like a cornered animal desperate to escape.

"I'm not going to hurt you." Vincent held up his hands to show he was unarmed.

Ravi's shoulders relaxed, but only slightly. "Then why are you here?"

"We came back to rescue you," Vincent said. "That is, if you all want to escape."

Ravi shrugged. "I've been here loads longer than the rest of them. And the Lady punishes anyone who attempts to escape. They might be too scared to try."

"I guess we'll find out." Vincent held the door open for Ravi.

In minutes, all the kids were out of their cells, whispering and watching Vincent and Georgia warily.

"So what's the plan?" Benjamin spoke up. "Are we going to fight the Lady? I can help."

A few of the older kids nodded.

"I don't want to get beat up like Ravi," a skinny boy chimed in.

Several kids cringed at this comment.

"No one is fighting or getting beat up," Vincent said. "We brought a way out with us."

Georgia held up the miniature. The lace-collared man's sly smile seemed to say this was all a game. "You are going to follow me into this painting. It will be a tight fit when you first hop in, but just step left or right through the gray wall into the Corridor, and I'll show you the way from there."

"But where are we going to go?" Tanisha asked, a tremble in her voice.

Georgia bent down and took her hand. "Somewhere safe, where Lili is. Then, hopefully, home to your parents. You can hold my hand, okay?"

Tanisha nodded and gripped Georgia's hand.

"Ready?" she asked as she propped the tiny painting against the wall. Then she and Tanisha disappeared into the miniature. The other kids looked around hesitantly, but eventually Benjamin stepped forward and followed. One by one, the other kids crossed into the painting.

Vincent kept an eye on the door. His foot tapped nervously, reminding him his feet were bare. His shoes were still by the dragon. He didn't know what his aunt could do with a painting connected to him, but leaving it seemed like a bad idea.

Vincent glanced back to see that Ravi was the only kid left in the room. He was watching Vincent through narrowed eyes.

"What?"

"Are you really here *just* to rescue us?" Ravi asked.

"Why else?" Vincent said hastily. "Just hurry before we get caught."

With one last glance, Ravi stepped into the painting.

Vincent picked up the miniature. He could do this. It wouldn't take more than a minute.

He opened the door. No sound or movement in the

hallway. He reached the ornate red door without incident. It was slightly ajar. Had they forgotten to close it earlier? He peeked into the empty room and stepped inside. After creeping around the divider, he nestled the miniature on the floor between his shoes. Then he grabbed a palette, squirted out some paint, and loaded a brush.

He turned to the dragon and froze. He'd assumed it would be easy to destroy it. Jesus had given him a new vision of who he could be, but that dragon still lurked inside him. Painting over it wouldn't change that. Still, he couldn't leave it for Aunt Adelaide.

Maybe he could take it with him. He glanced around for a bag or case to hide it in. But when he saw the painting-lined walls, it hit him: They'd been looking for *The Potato Eaters* in the wrong place. *This* was where his aunt kept anything precious, where she had so much confidence that she even kept some paintings framed.

If *The Potato Eaters* was hidden here, maybe he could help Georgia prove herself to her parents. Maybe he could even prove himself to his own parents.

He still had time. He absentmindedly tucked the paintbrush into his back pocket as he started searching the room.

A thump behind him made him spin. Ravi stooped and picked up the miniature.

"Looking for something?"

"Give that back." Vincent held out his hand.

"I think I'll keep it until you tell me what's really going on." Ravi scowled through bloodshot eyes. "You act like the hero, but you just want something. You're not any better than her. I may as well pick the winning team."

"That's not true," Vincent began, but Ravi shoved past and pounded on the only other door in the room.

It opened with a terrible slowness. Aunt Adelaide stood in a long scarlet dressing gown.

"My dear nephew." Adelaide's cold eyes glanced from his bare feet to the Rembrandt on her wall. She grimaced. "What a surprise."

25

"Why, exactly, are you here?" Aunt Adelaide asked.

"He stole the Wanderers." Ravi answered before Vincent had the chance. "They escaped through this." He handed the miniature to Aunt Adelaide.

"I see you've chosen your side." Her heels— apparently she didn't keep slippers by her bed—clicked quietly as she took one slow step after another. "I won't hold it against you, nephew. I know you're only doing what you think is right. Just like I am."

"What you're doing isn't right," Vincent said, taking a step back. "You can't just go around kidnapping people."

"Kidnapping?" She feigned shock. "Is that what you think? Oh, no, Vincent dearest, these children were lost. Lost in paintings. Lost in Corridors. I didn't kidnap them. I rescued them."

"Like you rescued that painting at the Van Gogh Museum?"

Aunt Adelaide smirked. "*Liberated* might be a better word, but yes. Art should belong to those who know how to use it. I know how to use it." She tilted her head and looked at Vincent as though he were a small child. "You're still so naïve. I know you'll come to view things my way once you see the Restorationists for what they really are—a silly family with a hero complex and no idea what to do with their power."

Vincent glanced at the miniature in her hand. Could he still escape?

"Clever." She examined the painting in her palm. "Was this your idea?"

He shrugged.

"Modest too." Aunt Adelaide tucked the portrait into the pocket of her robe. If Georgia came looking for him, could she Travel through if it was covered up? Vincent didn't think so. It would explain why Uncle Leo kept the paintings upstairs covered with sheets.

Vincent studied his aunt. She looked so much like his mom, yet she was utterly different from her. Mom may have kept the truth from him—shielded him from the world even when he didn't want her to—but she made him feel safe. His aunt didn't hide the truth from him, but she twisted it somehow. She felt dangerous.

But maybe that shiftiness could work to Vincent's advantage.

"If you really want me to believe you aren't a bad guy, prove it," he said.

She arched an eyebrow. "How should I do that?"

"Return *The Potato Eaters*."

Adelaide chuckled. "Look at you exerting your power. You'll be one of us yet."

Vincent shuffled his bare feet. "Well?"

"I don't think you realize the position you are in," she said. "You may have gotten two of my employees arrested during your escape. And you may have taken the children—for now. But I'm the one with the knowledge, the paintings, the backup."

Adelaide walked to the buzzer and pressed it with one manicured finger. A few minutes later, Tight Braids, her hair loose and wavy, along with the teacher with the wispy goatee, stumbled into the room.

"Pack up the Rembrandt, and proceed to the safe house," Aunt Adelaide directed. "I had hoped to enjoy it for a few more hours before the sale, but I can't risk more people tracking water into my rooms."

"What about the children?" Tight Braids asked as Goatee hurried to remove the painting from the wall.

"Gone," Aunt Adelaide said with a careless flick of her wrist. "Gather the rest of the team, and go. We'll catch up. Ravi?" She motioned toward her room, and the boy scurried into it.

She then turned to Vincent. "What to do with you, dear nephew?" She tapped her lip and took a step toward him. "I'm the only one who can train you. You have so much potential, and yet you've caused so much trouble. You remind me of myself."

Vincent shuddered. Aunt Adelaide made it sound like joining her was inevitable. Like destiny. He didn't want to be anything like her. That ugly dragon proved he had the potential for evil in his heart. But he didn't have to use his art that way. Didn't he have a choice in the matter? He remembered Lilias Trotter, who'd left her chance at fame to go help people. The glowing hand, which had written on the wall to put an end to evil. Jesus, who had calmly woken in the middle of a boat-sinking storm. What was it Georgia had said? Fear shouldn't get to decide what he would do.

Ravi returned, a rectangular black case in his arms. It had to be *The Potato Eaters*.

"Ideally, I'd send you home," Adelaide said. "Let you realize that Leo's just a foolish old man and that my sister was never very skilled to begin with. We could have kept this little gateway open for you to come visit me."

She pulled the miniature from her pocket.

That was when Georgia appeared.

"What's the holdup?" She turned, taking in the rest of the room. "Aunt Artemisia?"

"Wrong, dear. Perhaps your cousin can catch you up." Adelaide swept past Vincent. Ravi trailed behind her, still holding the case containing *The Potato Eaters*. She paused at the exit, tucked the miniature back into her pocket, then patted it while eyeing Vincent. "I'll be patient."

"What's going on?" Georgia looked frantically between the empty doorway and Vincent.

He grabbed her arm. "This is your chance to prove to your parents that you're ready. We can get that painting back."

She jerked her arm back. "From your mom? Did you know she was a Distortionist or whatever this whole time?"

"It's not my mom. It's her twin, Adelaide," Vincent explained, his words tumbling out. "She didn't die in the fire. She's the Lady running this whole place. I shouldn't have kept that secret, but we still have a chance to stop them. Hurry!"

Vincent ran down the hallway and caught sight of Ravi disappearing into the conference room. He glanced back to find Georgia just standing in the hallway, arms crossed.

"Why would you lie to me?"

"It's not like you were exactly honest with me," he said, walking back toward her.

"I was just showing off, but you . . ." She shook her head. "I don't get it."

Vincent ran his fingers through his hair. "I don't know why. I was confused—about a lot of things. I messed up big time, and I'm sorry. I should have trusted you. But they're getting away with the painting and our only way out. Isn't that more important?"

Georgia studied him for a short moment, then nodded. "Fine."

Three framed paintings sat propped against the wall in the conference room: Two Vincent didn't recognize, but the third was the van Gogh where they had first met Ravi.

"Should we split up?" Vincent asked. There was no way to know which painting his aunt and Ravi had Traveled through.

"Let me think." Georgia's eyes darted from one painting to the next. "Let's stick with van Gogh. We know they have access to the Met. That could be where they're headed. And these two"—she gestured toward the others—"these artists aren't at the Met."

"Navigation really is a superpower. Come on." Vincent stepped toward *Landscape in the Neighbourhood of Saint-Rémy,* but Georgia stopped him.

"Wait. There could be a trap. Let's be ready."

Vincent swallowed hard, remembering the training with never-ending holes. They wouldn't have harnesses this time. Surely his aunt wouldn't set that kind of trap for him. Even so, Vincent reached for the satchel, then froze. Things had been so chaotic, he hadn't realized it was lighter than it should be. He opened the flap and removed its only contents: a single palette knife.

"This is all that's left." He handed the knife to Georgia with a grimace. "The rest of the tools are at the bottom of the sea by now."

"Well, we can't wait any longer," she said. "You sure you're ready to risk your life for art?"

Vincent set his jaw and nodded. "Isn't that what being a Restorationist is all about?"

"So you're a Restorationist now?" She raised an eyebrow, the hint of a grin on her face.

"I'd like to be." He spoke almost without thinking and was surprised to find it was true.

Georgia held out her hand. "Together."

They grasped hands, took a deep breath, then stepped into the painting.

And fell into darkness.

26

Vincent's right arm nearly jerked out of socket. The palette knife plummeted past his face, growing smaller and smaller as it fell into the hole, never seeming to reach the bottom of the endless darkness.

He looked up at Georgia, who clung to the edge of the black hole with one hand, her other gripping his own.

Aunt Adelaide peered down at them. "This is not what I wanted, nephew. We could still do great things together. Join me."

Vincent's jaw clenched. What could he do? If he didn't say yes, they would die, not just here in the painting but for real. Maybe they would smash on a rocky bottom. Or maybe they would fall for days until they died of dehydration. Either way, no one would ever know what had

happened to them. This was about to be game over, and he wouldn't get a replay.

His sweaty hand began to slip in Georgia's grasp, and she grunted. She wouldn't be able to hold on forever.

If he had only thought to catch that palette knife. Or if he had a brush, he could at least try to create a handhold.

A brush!

He reached into his back pocket with his free hand and pulled out the one he had absentmindedly stashed there. It was still gooey with paint.

Except . . . he wasn't left-handed. To have a chance, he needed his right. He needed Georgia to . . .

"Let me go," he whispered.

"What?" She looked down at him in horror. "No way. We'll figure this out."

"Nephew, we can make a deal," Aunt Adelaide cajoled. "You can have anything you want. I'll even spare your cousin if she means so much to you. Just say yes, and Ravi will throw down a rope."

"Trust me." Vincent started to slide his fingers from his cousin's hand. She wouldn't be able to hold on much longer anyway. He gave her a reassuring nod. "Remember, fear doesn't get to decide."

Georgia let out one convulsive sob, shut her eyes, and opened her hand.

Time seemed to slow as Vincent plummeted deeper into the hole of inky paint. He was surrounded by the one thing an Artist needed.

Vincent swiped his brush across the side of the hole. It took a few tries to create a handhold, but he finally did it and held on even as his fingertips chafed painfully. He then reached as low as he could and painted a wide ledge to stand on.

He looked up at the circle of light high above him. Georgia still held on. Without him weighing her down, she had a better chance of climbing out.

Vincent painted a net across the shaft to catch her—or himself—just in case. He tested it with his weight, and it seemed to hold. Good.

Now, how to get back quickly?

He could paint more handholds or a ladder, but that would take ages to climb. Could he paint a balloon or a bird to carry him out of the hole?

Vincent suddenly remembered what the round-faced painting instructor had said: An Artist could over-come the forced perspective within a painting. His five senses might be telling him otherwise, but a painting wasn't actually three-dimensional. This depth, this hole, was just an illusion on a flat surface. And if that was true . . .

Vincent pointed the brush at a spot above him and painted, not worrying whether or not the paint touched a surface. Widely set side rails narrowed to meet each other near the top of the hole. He painted three steps to connect the rails and began climbing his ladder, brush clenched between his teeth. In a moment, he was scrambling out of the hole.

At the top he found Aunt Adelaide, who gawked at him while Ravi scurried backward.

Keeping the principles of forced perspective in mind, Vincent pointed his brush at his aunt. It didn't matter that it didn't physically touch her. The paint behaved as he directed it, tying her arms to her sides.

Aunt Adelaide's eyes bulged. "Nephew. I'm so relieved." She managed to keep her voice smooth with only a slight tremor. "Ravi was a naughty boy to make that hole. Surely now you see that I must be the one to train you. There is only—"

Vincent swiped a gag across her mouth. "No more lies." He turned to Ravi. "Hand over the painting."

Ravi set the painting at Vincent's feet before backing away again. He looked like a scared rabbit, and Vincent wavered on what to do with him. Should he give him another chance and take Ravi home with them? Ravi had acted out of fear, and Vincent understood fear. Fear had led him to a lot of bad decisions—lying to Georgia, not rescuing the other kids the first time—but it had also kept Vincent from embracing art as the gift it was.

"Vincent!" Georgia screamed. "I can't hold on!"

He turned to see her disappear down the hole.

Vincent dove to the ground, searching for her in the blackness. Had the net held? It was only paint, after all.

"I'm okay!" Georgia's voice echoed up to him.

He sighed in relief. "Do you see the ladder?"

"Yes, but the rungs—"

"Just try it. It will work."

Moments later, Georgia was hugging him and crying into his shoulder. "I thought I was dead. I thought we were both dead."

"I know." Vincent squeezed her back. "There's one thing Aunt Adelaide was right about. I need training. We both do."

Georgia pulled back and looked around. "Where is she?"

There was no sign of either his aunt or Ravi. But the stolen painting still lay on the ground where Ravi had set it.

"Should we go after them?" Vincent asked.

"Yesterday I might have said yes. But now I don't

really feel like I need to prove myself." Georgia smiled at him. "I think I just needed someone to believe in me."

Vincent's ears grew warm. He tucked the paintbrush back into his pocket and looked around the painting. "We'll have to clean this up, even if we can't take it with us. I wouldn't want anyone else to fall into that hole."

Georgia punched him playfully on the shoulder. "Now that's thinking like a real Restorationist."

Vincent smiled. A few days ago, the last thing he'd wanted was to have anything to do with art. But now he really did want to be a Restorationist. He hadn't chosen it—it was more like it had chosen him. But would his parents agree?

Once they'd restored the painting as best they could, he said, "Well, we lost the miniature, so I hope you have some convoluted method of navigating us home."

Georgia grinned. "There's always a backup plan."

27

Uncle Leo had found spots for the sixteen extra kids to bunk, spread around the house on couches, chairs, and blankets on the floor.

Vincent and Georgia tiptoed through the maze of sleeping kids and found Uncle Leo in his studio. He was on the phone but visibly relaxed when he saw them and waved them over for a hug.

"All right. See you tomorrow." He clicked the phone onto the receiver. "Thank God," he said, turning to Vincent and Georgia. "When y'all didn't make it back . . . Well, I'm just glad y'all did make it back."

"Us too," Vincent said. He'd never been so happy to be anywhere.

"I gave away y'all's beds." Uncle Leo rubbed the back of his neck and yawned. "Mine too."

"I'm not sure I could sleep anyway," Vincent said.

"Was that my parents on the phone?" Georgia asked in a hesitant voice.

Uncle Leo shook his head. "FBI. I've got a contact from the old days. Lucky she still works there. She's going to come sort out what to do with these kids."

"Gramps, they can all Travel," Georgia said. "We could start our own training school for them. We'd finally have a fighting chance against the Distortionists."

It made a lot of sense. They needed more people if they were going to go up against the Distortionists—and whatever Aunt Adelaide was doing. But thinking of Aunt Adelaide reminded Vincent that these kids had been snatched from their families.

"We can't keep them here," Vincent said.

"You're darn right," Uncle Leo said. "I don't have the room."

"I mean, we can't keep them at all," Vincent corrected. "These kids were kidnapped. They have families who miss them. If we kept them, we wouldn't be any better than . . . We'd be kidnappers ourselves."

Uncle Leo stroked his mustache. "That's thinking like a true Restorationist."

It was the second time today Vincent had received this compliment. He was sure he couldn't think of a better one.

"Oh!" Georgia said suddenly and plopped the black

case onto Uncle Leo's worktable. "We also recovered a painting!"

Uncle Leo opened the case and whistled through his teeth. "I'm sure proud of you kids." His eyes were shining. Then he laughed. "We're going to have to come up with one heck of a story to explain sixteen kids and a stolen painting to the FBI."

"All in a day's work, right, Gramps?"

"I reckon so."

True to her word, Uncle Leo's FBI friend arrived mid-morning.

"Let me get this straight." Agent Jiménez eyed Uncle Leo skeptically after listening to his wild story. "You want me to buy that a Mexican cartel truck broke down and that sixteen kids in matching pajamas escaped with a painting that was stolen in Europe a few days ago?"

If she had trouble believing that, she'd never buy the actual truth. Uncle Leo had already coached the kids on the story he'd concocted and made it clear they were not to try Traveling again or tell anyone about it.

"I get it," Uncle Leo said, holding up his hands. "I'd

think it was a tall tale, too, but where'd all these kids come from? It's not like they just magically appeared."

The agent nodded. "And where's the truck?"

"Hightailed it out of here."

"You always were a wily one, Leo." She grinned. "It's good to see you again."

"Raquel, I gotta ask you a favor." His voice broke. "If you can't locate their parents, for even one of them . . ."

"I'll let you know." She gave his shoulder a pat and turned to leave.

"See you later," Benjamin said, giving Vincent a fist bump.

"Yeah." Vincent grinned. "I hope so."

Uncle Leo had given each kid his business card and the promise that when they were older, any of them could come to him to train as a Restorationist if they wanted. Vincent had a feeling that Benjamin would be the first to reach out.

Lili and Tanisha clung to each other until it was time for Tanisha to climb into one of the black SUVs.

Once the kids were gone, Uncle Leo clapped his hands. "Time to tidy up. Lili, you start folding blankets upstairs."

"Okay!" She ran off, accompanied by Mr. Rumples.

"You two can help down here, but first, where's the old tool kit you took from the closet?"

Vincent cringed. "I lost it. But I have the satchel."

Uncle Leo sighed. He looked at Georgia. "The canoe?"

"Gone."

"It's all right." Uncle Leo patted Georgia's shoulder. "At least y'all brought back the miniature. That's why y'all came home the back way, right?" Georgia had asked Uncle Leo to frame another painting last night before she went back in.

Vincent bit his lip. Using the miniatures had been his idea, and he felt responsible. "Actually, we lost that too. I could pay you back. It can't have been worth that much. It was only a few inches big."

Uncle Leo's bushy eyebrows shot up. "Not worth . . ." he stammered. "Well, if you think 9,000 pounds isn't that much."

Vincent shot a glance at Georgia. "How much is 9,000 pounds?"

"Over $10,000," she said. Vincent's mouth dropped open. "Sorry, Gramps. How can we make it up to you?"

"I'm just relieved y'all are okay," Uncle Leo said, waving off their concern. "The loss of art is always tragic, but your lives—and the lives of those kids y'all saved—are worth a whole lot more than any painting." He sighed and rubbed his eyes. "But I reckon I need help sorting out what I'm going to tell y'all's folks when they get back. If they knew I—"

"Vincent's an Artist," Georgia interrupted.

Vincent froze, unsure what to say. He'd barely accepted the fact for himself.

"Come again?" Uncle Leo sputtered.

"You should have seen what he did in the van Gogh— and the Rembrandt!" Georgia continued. "You *have* to train him, Gramps! When was the last time there was an Artist in the family?"

"If that's the case, this does change things." Uncle Leo stared down at him appraisingly, and Vincent felt his ears grow hot. Still, maybe it was good that Uncle Leo knew. Maybe he could help convince Vincent's mom to let him train.

"I know, right?" Georgia grinned like she'd been given a new puppy.

"Artemisia will have to reconsider . . . that is, if she didn't already figure . . ." Uncle Leo stroked his bushy mustache. "I've got some thinking to do." He turned and walked into his studio, not even bothering to shut the door.

Vincent glanced at Georgia. "Thanks for not mentioning you-know-who."

"It's not my secret to tell." She bit her lip. "But I'm not sure you should keep it hidden. I'm still mad at you for not telling me."

"I know." Vincent stared at his feet. He'd still

managed to forget his shoes. "I should have trusted you. I do trust you. But don't you think that finding out his niece is alive and a criminal would tear Uncle Leo up, not to mention my mom?"

"They aren't little kids who need protecting. They deserve the truth. Just like you deserved the truth."

Vincent sighed. "I'll think about it."

28

rring-brring. Uncle Leo's rotary telephone echoed from the studio.

Vincent set down his paintbrush, and Georgia stopped her wheel's spinning. Lili kept right on hand-sculpting a small clay figure. Evening light streamed through the picture window of the enclosed porch where they sat.

"Hello?" Uncle Leo's gruff voice came clearly through the open door. "Already? No, not a problem. They know. I'll explain in a bit."

Uncle Leo stepped onto the enclosed porch, a smile spreading across his face. "They're on their way."

Vincent and Georgia followed him to the living room. He stooped down and slid a flat black case from under the couch. Another painting.

In a few minutes, Georgia was hugging the two people now standing in front of them.

"We missed you so much, mija!" the woman said. She was taller than Georgia with long dark brown hair and olive skin.

"You'll be old enough to come on a mission with us soon—I promise," said the man with Georgia's same wild red hair, only a shade brighter.

Georgia pulled away, cheeks flushed. "Well . . ." she began, but then her parents noticed Vincent.

"Oh, you must be Vincent. I'm Edward, your mom's cousin." Georgia's dad held out his hand, and Vincent shook it.

"I'm your tía Frida." She embraced Vincent in a tight hug.

Beep-beep.

"What in tarnation?" Uncle Leo hurried to the front door. The rest of the party followed.

Moments later, Vincent's parents were bustling into the house. "We're back early!"

"Mommy!" Lili came barreling in from the back porch, her hands still wet with clay. She practically knocked Mom over with her momentum, but Dad steadied them.

"I thought y'all weren't coming in till tomorrow," Uncle Leo said.

"We decided not to stay the night in Galveston after

all. We missed the kids, so we just drove straight here." Vincent's mom took in the group gathered before her. Her eyes filled with tears.

"Eddie! I didn't see a car . . ." She trailed off, then turned to Uncle Leo with a look of betrayal. "You promised."

"It's not his fault." Vincent stepped forward. "And it's not Georgia's either. Lili went into a painting on accident, and we had to get her back."

His mom stifled a gasp behind her hand. Vincent couldn't help but notice how different her whole demeanor was from her sister's. How had he ever mistaken the two?

The whole story, minus any mentions of Aunt Adelaide, poured from Vincent with some help from Georgia and interjections from Lili along the way. By the time he finished, they were all seated in the living room and Uncle Leo was handing everyone tall glasses of iced tea.

"Well, I'm just glad it's all over and you're safe," Mom said.

"That's just it." Vincent squirmed in his seat. "There are things going on—bad things—and I can help." He paused, looking his parents in the eye. "Maybe some things are more important than being safe."

"But you're just a kid," Dad protested.

"Jeffery." Uncle Leo patted Dad's shoulder. "He's an Artist."

"Well, we know that. That's why we wanted him to spend this week with you."

"No, I mean"—Uncle Leo looked significantly at each of the adults—"he's an *Artist*."

Uncle Edward stood, Tía Frida mumbled something in Spanish, and Vincent's mom grasped his hand, eyes welling with more tears.

"Uncle Leo, are you sure?" Mom asked. "There hasn't been an Artist in the family for generations."

"Or in any Restorationist family," Tía Frida chimed in.

Georgia quickly described how Vincent had fixed the canoe in *The Storm on the Sea of Galilee* and overcome the forced perspective to save them both in *Landscape in the Neighbourhood of Saint-Rémy*. Hearing the details again bolstered Vincent's determination to make his request.

"I want to train," he said. "Starting this summer. I only gave up painting because I was afraid I'd never be good enough, but now I understand that's not the point of art. I'm part of this, like it or not. And so is Lili somehow. I need to know how to navigate this world so that we don't have to be afraid."

Uncle Edward leaned over and squeezed Mom's shoulder. "He's right, you know."

"And I want to go on missions," Georgia said. "I'm ready."

"Touché." He ruffled her hair. "I think you just might be."

Vincent's mom nodded slowly and squeezed his hand. "We thought we could keep you safe by keeping this world secret, but it found you anyway. I guess I always knew you would eventually. If something were to happen again, I'd at least want you prepared."

Vincent looked up at his dad, who nodded his approval. "I have to trust your mom on this one." Vincent beamed.

"Well, if you wanted training, don't you think you should have asked me?" Uncle Leo raised a bushy eyebrow, but the corner of his mouth twitched in a secret smile, and everyone laughed.

"There's just one thing I need before we do any training." Vincent held up a bare foot. "New shoes."

Everyone laughed. Maybe they really could be a family all together, making art and fighting evil. At least he'd have a chance to find out.

Lili plopped a notebook in Vincent's lap. "Draw with me." She held out a pencil.

Vincent took it, his mind spinning with ideas: things he wanted to draw and paint, things he wanted to try out inside a painting, paintings he wanted to Travel to.

When they got home, maybe he'd ask his mom to tell him about her sister and ask her again why they'd hidden everything for so long. Maybe they'd even Travel together. He'd definitely ask her to paint with him again—like they used to.

But whatever happened with Traveling and training as a Restorationist, this was one way, right now, that he could be the person he was meant to be. That he could accept art as a gift.

He grinned at his sister. "What should we draw?"

AUTHOR'S NOTE

When I first started writing *Beneath the Swirling Sky* in 2020, I wondered if a book centered on art was out of touch and irrelevant. Yet the last few years have seen the rise in NFTs, AI-created art with all the controversy surrounding it, and popular exhibits where van Gogh's art is projected on the walls. Unfortunately, we've also seen a rise in threatening protesters who, as a platform for their message, have thrown harmful items at priceless masterpieces.

Art is powerful. And that's never been more evident than today. Art draws on our emotions. Creating and enjoying art are part of what makes us human. In fact, I'd argue that the urge to create is one way we exhibit the image of God. The art we've been handed from previous generations is part of our history. The best art helps us engage with truth, whether it's about remembering beauty or showing us our flaws. As long as there are people, art will always be important.

I'm not a visual artist myself, but I identify with Vincent's journey nonetheless. As a kid, I started writing poetry almost as soon as I could hold a pencil. In fourth grade, I began writing my first novel, sure that creating stories for other kids was what I was meant to do. But by the time I reached middle school, I'd given in to the fear that I wasn't good enough. I didn't write another story until I had kids of my own.

I've heard another author say that, on school visits, she'll ask the kids, "Who here is an artist?" In second grade, all the hands shoot up. But by fifth grade, only the rare kid will raise their hand. This book is for all the kids, like me and Vincent, who are afraid to claim their status as an artist, writer, or creator of any kind.

Art has been a part of my life since childhood. My mom was an art teacher, and my grandparents' home was a veritable museum of art, sculpture, and trinkets from around the world. It was without a doubt the most magical place from my childhood. Perhaps that's why I couldn't think of a better setting for this story, though I've relocated their house to the middle of the Texas countryside.

When I figured out this story would be part of the "real world," I did my best to make the art part as realistic as possible. Every painting, to the best of my research at the time I was writing, is depicted in its actual location, though of course museums rearrange and lend paintings. All the paintings in Uncle Leo's house are privately owned—other than *Starry Night,* which belongs to the Museum of Modern Art in New York and is meant to be at Uncle Leo's for restoration. All paintings owned by Adelaide are publicly known to be stolen. The trickiest bit of realism was accurately depicting the layout of the Van Gogh Museum in Amsterdam, a location I've experienced only through their website and Google Street View.

One thing I've fudged on is museum security. While museum guards are notoriously underpaid, most museums now have forms of electronic security, which I've ignored for the purpose of this story. However, if you've read as many true stories of art thefts as I have, you might conclude that alarms and guards are less effective than one might hope.

Art theft is a fascinating topic to research, and it led me down several rabbit holes. Sadly, I've learned that most stolen art is never recovered. Some of it really does go to fund terrorism. And much of it is likely destroyed when thieves find it harder to sell than they assumed.

My grandparents experienced a rather dramatic art theft in 1984, when I was four years old. They owned an art gallery on the San Antonio River Walk. The most prominent piece displayed was a group of soldiers painted by Norman Rockwell entitled *Are We Downhearted?* One day, two thieves walked in, cut the painting from the frame with a box cutter, and ran. Although the FBI got involved, the painting was never recovered. Cutting paintings from frames with a box cutter is the same technique used by the two thieves (disguised as cops) in the notorious Gardner Museum theft a few years later in 1990, which remains the largest art heist in history. *The Storm on the Sea of Galilee*, Rembrandt's only seascape, which Vincent and Georgia Travel through, was stolen in that heist.

One more note about nudity in art. If you look up any of the artists mentioned or check out books from the library about them or even if you visit a museum, you are likely to come across some paintings or sketches of nudes. There are lots of reasons for this, but as Georgia says, "Naked people are a part of art." That doesn't mean you have to look at any art that makes you uncomfortable. You may not have a canoe to cover your head with like Vincent, but you could have a parent help you when searching for images, and you can always look away when you come across something you didn't want to see. There's so much great art out there, and I'd hate for you to miss it just to avoid those few.

PAINTINGS AND ARTISTS REFERENCED IN THIS WORK

PAINTINGS YOU CAN VISIT AT A MUSEUM:

- *Starry Night*, Vincent van Gogh, the Museum of Modern Art, New York City (seen at Uncle Leo's)
- *Wheatfield with Crows*, Vincent van Gogh, the Van Gogh Museum, Amsterdam
- *Water Mill at Gennep*, Vincent van Gogh, the Van Gogh Museum, Amsterdam
- *Self-Portrait with Pipe*, Vincent van Gogh, the Van Gogh Museum, Amsterdam
- *Irises*, Vincent van Gogh, the Van Gogh Museum, Amsterdam
- *Nursery on Schenkweg*, Vincent van Gogh, the Met, New York City

- *Corridor in the Asylum,* Vincent van Gogh, the Met, New York City

- *St. Jerome Reading,* Rembrandt, the Met, New York City

- *The Potato Eaters,* Vincent van Gogh, the Van Gogh Museum, Amsterdam

- *Expressman,* Norman Rockwell, the Met, New York City

- *Belshazzar's Feast,* Rembrandt, the National Gallery, London

- *The Sunken Path,* Jules Dupré, the Van Gogh Museum, Amsterdam

- M. C. Escher's drawings are referenced, but no particular one is depicted. However, I highly recommend checking out a library book of his fascinating work.

PRIVATELY OWNED PAINTINGS SEEN AT UNCLE LEO'S HOUSE:

- *Nature Forms—Gaspé,* Georgia O'Keeffe

- *Self-Portrait Very Ugly,* Frida Kahlo

- *Woman with a Red Umbrella Seated in Profile,* Henri Matisse

- *Sous-bois à Fontainebleau*, Paul Cézanne

- *Repairing Stained Glass*, Norman Rockwell

- *Portrait of a Gentleman, Circa 1590*, Nicholas Hilliard

- *Portrait of a Lady, Circa 1605*, Nicholas Hilliard

STOLEN PAINTINGS YET TO BE RECOVERED:

- *Landscape in the Neighbourhood of Saint-Rémy*, Vincent van Gogh

- *The Storm on the Sea of Galilee*, Rembrandt

The locations of paintings are based on research done during the time of the writing of this book. Museums often loan their art, rearrange their pieces, or remove certain works for restoration or to make room for others. Because of this, the works may not currently be on display at the locations listed.

ACKNOWLEDGMENTS

To my grandparents, George and Josephine. Your house was magical in so many ways, but certainly the art on the walls (and cram-stacked in that upstairs room) opened a door in my mind that led to this story. I wish y'all were around to read it. And to my mom, Jeanie, for encouraging an interest in art without ever pressuring me.

To Sam Smith, for being the first non-family member to believe in this project. For giving me the courage to talk about it, and for your generosity in time and story insights. Glenn McCarty, for being my critique partner and the second person (after my oldest daughter) to read this book. And to James Witmer, for your constant faith in my ability to pull this off.

To Sheri, and the Turner crew, for your wonderful descriptions of New York pizza. Even though I had to cut those scenes from the final draft, I find myself hoping

I can use them elsewhere (or at least eat some of that pizza one day). And to Sheri, for your pottery expertise! Georgia is a fuller character because of you.

To James, for taking the time to give this a read as my pastor. I appreciate your advice and thoughtfulness. And to you and Catie, for giving me a quiet place to write during VBS.

Speaking of places to write, lots of work took place at LearningRx while my girls had tutoring. Thanks for all the coffee!

To the Six Chicks, for all your encouragement. Sarah, whose insight into my book proposal is the whole reason this project was discovered. Rachel, for agreeing to be one of my beta readers. Kathleen, for answering my TESOL-related questions. Letty, for your constant faith that "you've got this." Stephanie, for your encouragement from across the country.

To my teen beta readers, Ava, Aryn, Sophia, and Caleb. I so appreciate you taking the time to read my story in the middle of a busy school year. Your encouragement has given me confidence that this story will resonate with its target audience!

To my friend Mindy, for confirming California details that I couldn't remember from my time living there while in college.

To my fellow authors Emma Fox, for your expert

advice on all things art, and Summer Rachel Short and Helena Sorensen, for your input and encouragement.

To the Rabbit Room's Hutchmoot conference in 2017. Russ Ramsey's talk on van Gogh reawakened my connection with his art, and Jennifer Trafton and Lanier Ivester's session introduced me to Lilias Trotter, who Lili was named after.

To my amazing agent, Keely Boeving, for seeing the potential in this project before it was even finished and helping it find a home.

To my brilliant editor, Bunmi Ishola, for your excitement from the beginning and for the way you've pushed me on every detail of this story. This book would not be the same without your input!

Special thanks to WaterBrook publisher, Laura Barker, and editorial assistant, Luverta Reames. To everyone in production and design at Penguin Random House who has helped make this book so much better than I could have on my own: Abby Duval, Kayla Fenstermaker (whom I'm especially in awe of), Marysarah Quinn, Ashley Tucker, Jen Valero, Phil Leung, Jessica Heim, Liza Stepanovich, and Chris Tanigawa. My name may be on the cover, but each of you contributed to this book in essential ways. Thank you! To the fantastic marketing and publicity team, Elizabeth Groening, Ada Ramos, Levi Phillips, and Jessica Kastner Keene, thank you for all the time and energy you put into getting the word out so kids can engage with this story. And to everyone else at PRH who has had a hand in this project, thank you from the bottom of my heart!

To my amazingly talented illustrator Vivienne To, I'm still pinching myself that you said yes to this book! I don't visualize faces, so seeing Vincent and Georgia (with even the clay/paint mark across her cheek) for the first time felt like meeting them all over again. Thank you for truly bringing this story to life!

To my husband, Demetrios. You saw me as a writer before I saw myself as one. You've constantly encouraged me, given me the time and space needed, and never flagged in your belief in me. Thank you. And to my kids. Caelyn, you were my first reader when this book was a mess and Vincent was a jerk (or more of a jerk), but you saw the story's potential. Thank you for your encouragement. And to Campbell, Everly, and Arden, thank you for always wanting to hear more about this story and for begging me to read it to you!

And finally, to Jesus. In 2020, I gave up on thinking I could do publishing my way and make it work. Your hand was so clear in leading me and this book where it needed to go. I'm praying that it works in readers' hearts the way only art can.

ABOUT THE AUTHOR

CAROLYN LEILOGLOU is the granddaughter of art collectors, daughter of an art teacher, and home-schooling mom to four wildly creative kids. She's the award-winning author of the picture book *Library's Most Wanted,* and her poems and short stories have appeared in children's magazines around the world. You can find her at carolynleiloglou.com.

ABOUT THE ILLUSTRATOR

VIVIENNE TO is a New Zealand–based illustrator and visual development artist. She has designed several animated feature films and created illustrations for many middle-grade books. When she isn't drawing, Vivienne can be found knitting on the couch, watching cute dogs at the local park, or reading in the children's section of the library.

Sneak Peek from

BETWEEN FLOWERS AND BONES

THE RESTORATIONISTS

BOOK 2

Georgia stopped in front of the window to their first destination. The bright backlit colors of the painting made her squint, almost as if this were a real sunset shining into the darkness of the Corridor. *From the Plains I* looked like an enormous yellow sun dipping below the horizon, its edge curved in a jagged lightning-like arch.

"My mom considers that a safe painting?" Vincent asked, staring at the glowing window with obvious hesitation. "It looks like we'll be standing on the surface of the sun."

"I think 'safe' is more related to the fact that there aren't many stolen O'Keeffes"—only one that she was aware of—"so we shouldn't expect to run into any Distortionists. The sun's exaggerated, but the view is meant to be somewhere in Texas. We won't burn up."

"I've been burning up all week at Uncle Leo's."

Georgia smirked. "We haven't even hit triple digits yet."

"Why couldn't O'Keeffe have painted icebergs instead?"

"Come on." She reached toward the window, bracing herself for the heat as she entered the painting.

The sun was scorching, even if it was just made of paint. She squinted against its radiance and held up a hand to shield her face. The orange-and-red landscape lay flat and featureless, and the giant sun filled the horizon, looming over her.

"Let's get out of here," Vincent said. He turned toward the back wall of the painting, which held the framed window leading to the museum.

"Wait!" Georgia grabbed his arm and pulled him further into the painting. "We have to find the clue."

"How? There's nothing here but sun, and I'm not getting any closer."

She looked around helplessly. Where would her parents have hidden something? They wouldn't have wanted to get closer to the sun either.

She turned her back to the horizon so she could see better, then looked along the bright red ground. Farther along, closer to their exit, the ground darkened to maroon. Was it cooler as well?

"Come on." She strode forward, sweat trickling down her back, but the sun's heat seemed to lessen as she walked away from it.

The maroon ground was slightly cooler.

"What's that?" Vincent hurried to where a small envelope lay stark white against the dark ground. How had she missed that?

"Grab it, and we can read it in the museum." Georgia hurried to the window and peered out into the space beyond. It was a small room with brown brick floors, off-white walls, and a wood-paneled ceiling. In the corner across from them hung a few more paintings, including *Leaf Motif*, another O'Keeffe that would have been much more pleasant to Travel through.

The museum was practically empty but not completely, which actually made it trickier than if it had been crowded. People barely looked twice when she stepped from a painting into a room already full of people and movement. But if she and Vincent hopped out now, it would be hard to explain where they'd come from.

The painting they were in seemed to hang in a corner of a room. Two broad doorways were visible from Georgia's vantage point, but with the angle of the painting, she couldn't be sure the room on the right was vacant. A mom with three young kids was being pulled through the room in front of them by her oldest child, who barely even glanced at the paintings before moving on.

"Let's go," she said when the family exited. "There's a low railing about three feet from the painting. Just step long when you exit, and you should be fine."

She reached forward and stepped out of the painting, avoiding the shin-high railing. Vincent followed, landing with one foot on the railing, but he recovered his balance quickly. When she saw the open envelope in his hand, she wasn't surprised that he'd nearly tripped. He must have been trying to read the message as he stepped into the museum.

"Let me see." She leaned over his shoulder.

"Hold on," Vincent said, yanking the paper away. "My eyes haven't even adjusted yet. That sun was blinding."

"Then hand it over." She made another grab for it, but Vincent didn't let go. The paper ripped in half. Great.

Georgia stalked toward the other side of the room, where *Leaf Motif* hung, to examine her half of the note. Only then did she realize the room to their right wasn't empty.

A security guard was staring at them with wide eyes. He'd been in their blind spot but was way too close not to have seen them. Surely he'd just assume they'd come through the doorway at the other end of the room, even though he had a clear view of it.

Georgia looked away. Usually she could try to blend into the crowd if she thought he'd been see exiting a painting. But it was pretty hard to explain materializing into a corner of an empty room.

Vincent crossed to stand beside her and held out his piece of the clue.

She glanced back at the guard. He was an older man with crow's-feet around his eyes and salt-and-pepper hair. He was still staring at them, but he smiled at her and nodded. Maybe he'd already convinced himself he was seeing things. If he hadn't yet, he would later. No one would believe kids had stepped out of a painting.

Don't miss the next step in Georgia and Vincent's extraordinary journey as they learn that every Gift was made to fight the darkness in a world where paintings become portals and adventure lurks behind every canvas.